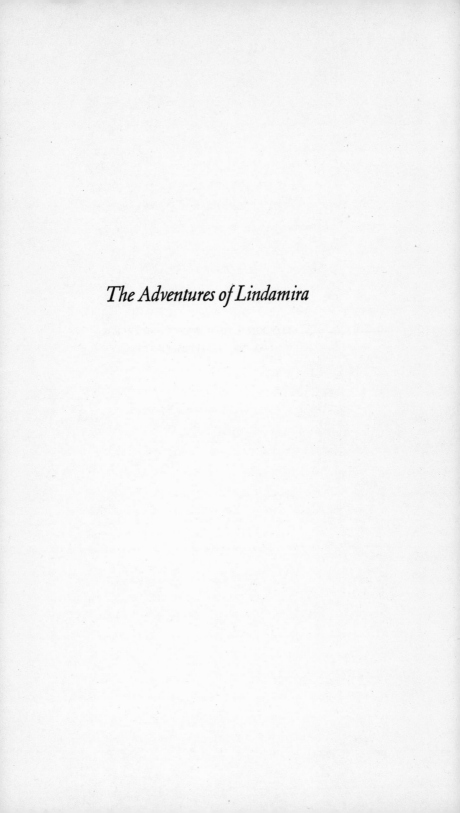

The Adventures of Lindamira

LONDON · GEOFFREY CUMBERLEGE
OXFORD UNIVERSITY PRESS

The Adventures of

LINDAMIRA

A Lady of Quality

edited by BENJAMIN BOYCE
THE UNIVERSITY OF NEBRASKA

UNIVERSITY OF MINNESOTA PRESS · MINNEAPOLIS

PRINTED AT THE NORTH CENTRAL PUBLISHING COMPANY, ST. PAUL

Editor's Introduction

Young lovers unhappily separated by fine feelings and selfish relatives; the influence upon art of that perpetually rising creature, the middle class; the question of how the English novel found nourishment at its roots — these are matters which the conscientious student of life and modern letters should not neglect. Yet few people have acquainted themselves with one of the important documents for such study, *The Adventures of Lindamira,* published in London in 1702. The explanation for the long neglect of this interesting little book is, I fear, the one given by Mr. D. B. Wyndham Lewis to account for his having ignored certain source books on François Villon — namely, that copies could be found only in libraries. It is to remedy such a lamentable state of affairs that the present edition of *Lindamira* is put forth.

There are several reasons, beyond the pleasure that its story might give, why *Lindamira* should be known. It is one of the earliest novels of English domestic life; it revealed, decades before *Pamela,* the value to the serious narrative artist of the epistolary pretense; nine years before Mr. Spectator phrased the need of tempering wit with morality and enlivening morality with wit *Lindamira* appeared in print doing almost that and appealing, as Mrs. Behn and Mrs. Manley notoriously did not do, to the tastes of genuinely respectable ladies; and not least, the book is a remarkable demonstration of how something of

v

situation, motivation, and sentiment could be abstracted from the now rather *démodé* French heroic romance and adapted to English middle-class life. Without *Lindamira* to show how the thing could happen, one might be disinclined to believe that the masculine stories of Defoe, the insistently bourgeois *Pamela,* and the hearty realism of Henry Fielding could all have been fostered by the foreign art of Madeleine de Scudéry.

The preface which Thomas Brown, a well-known journalist and satirist, wrote for the first edition of the volume Lord Ernle has called the manifesto of a new school of fiction. Without stressing the originality of the book Brown nonetheless made clear that the adventures to be related were set in familiar England, not in some remote land; that domestic life and civilized, virtuous London people, not foreign princes or town bullies, would provide the interest; and that the story was not "feigned" (the word was the usual one for flagrantly fictitious tales) but, rather, matter of fact. Whether Lindamira's story was actually true does not now matter, of course; in the Fourth Part the intricacy of the plotting makes one guess that there, at least, it was not true. But Brown in general gave his readers fair notice: laid on a bookseller's table beside any contemporary book of prose fiction, Congreve's recent *Incognita* not excepted, *Lindamira* was remarkable. Forty years before *Pamela* it offered a sketch of the theory and, with some romantic divagations, of the substance of the future, traditional English novel. The fact that the book was reissued in 1745 and 1751 when Richardson's and Fielding's novels were abroad suggests how much more "advanced" it was than most prose fiction of its day.

For many years, indeed for two centuries now, it has been the fashion to ridicule the heroic romances written in France in the seventeenth century. The laughter had already been heard in Brown's time. "Unnatural representations of the passions, false sentiments, false precepts, false wit, false honour, and false modesty," complained Mrs. Chapone in 1750, preferring the novels of her friend Mr. Richardson. Impossibly primitive warfare combined with impossibly delicate, introspective aristocrats, complains a modern critic. What chiefly is wrong with *Artamène ou le Grand Cyrus* (1649-1653) and *Clélie* (1654-1660) — and this the author of *Lindamira* perceived — is the improbable incidents, the unrelaxed *préciosité* of the style, and the exhaustingly grand dimensions of everything. But much in these works is true, human, universal, and this our author salvaged, applying everywhere in her construction the scale of one inch to Scudéry's yard.

Take the matter of situation and motivation. The "horrid Rigors of a long Absence," often occurring in the romances just when a lover stands on the threshold of victory, appear four times in *Lindamira,* sufficiently but not excrutiatingly prolonged. The heroic battles and kidnapings that accompany such torments are omitted in *Lindamira.* "False sentiments, false precepts . . . false honour"? Not wholly false, even in an increasingly busy and commercial society where, frankly, money counted but was not superabundant and yet where the pursuit of it in an actual job was still damaging to the reputation of a gentleman. Hence Lindamira's feeling that she must not interpose herself between Cleomidon and his wealthy uncle.

But fine feelings, the delicate counterpoise of admiration and thoughtfulness for one's friends and respect for oneself, the upsurge of the emotions and the restraint of good form — these are familiar in any civilized society, whether that of the *salons* of Paris or that of middle-class people in English town and country. Standards of honor, wit, modesty, and private heroism will be only partially altered, the greatest difference being in the setting and manners. Lindamira's powerful and mixed sensations when she first appears unmasked — and in a theater box — before a man she loves, her discomfiture when she learns that he is married, her unconquerable loyalty to Cleomidon and the persisting discrimination between her love for him and her warm friendship for Harnando, all are "modernized," Anglicized, and abbreviated versions of typical situations of the heart in the heroic romances. And the pretty elmlined path and romantic well where Lindamira meets Cleomidon, the rustic grove where Harnando overhears her speak her lover's name to an answering echo were also brought from France but adjusted to more modest circumstances.

A good illustration of how the plot-material and the sentimental analysis of the *roman* could be naturalized in the English novel appears in the episode in Letter XIX describing the behavior of the jealous young Octavius. The origin of this passage seems to have been the autobiographical narrative in *Artamène* dealing with the suffering of Leontidas (printed with the heading "The Jealous Lover" in *Artamenes; or, The Grand Cyrus . . . Englished by F. G.,* 1690-1691, Part III, Book I). Lindamira takes the place of the philosopher Lanthas as counselor to the incurable; but it is a remark of Leontidas's troubled mistress that supplies her with one of her most telling observations ("I had rather marry a Man that hates me, than one that loves me with any ingredient of Jealousy in his Love" —*Artamenes,* page 200). In *Lindamira* the episode, augmented by the incident of the game of cards for local and domestic flavor, is less than half as long as in the romance, and the melancholy prince has become a petulant townsman.

Discussions of other theoretical questions of ethics and manners occur in the English book as in the French ones but always more briefly, more pointedly, and they look more natural. Lindamira's sketch on page 11 of the sort of man she could love illustrates the art of reducing a French yard to an inch. Only in the long *histoire* of Doralisa is there much of the leisureliness and the delicate humor of Scudéry's conversations.

In characterization and names as well as in incidents and analysis *Lindamira* owes something to the romances. The names, Lindamira indicates, are to conceal the identities of "real" people and places; unfortunately they may also have the effect upon a modern reader, unaccustomed to the usual romantic naming of characters in seventeenth-century literature, of disguising the English authenticity. The name of our confiding and, at first, girlish heroine belonged also to a sumptuous and dazzling princess in *Clélie* (Part III, Book II). Both Scudéry's lady and our Lindamira are endowed with virtue and courage; both are victims of machination; both meet a lover in an arbor. But these specifications are common to the heroines in seventeenth-century fiction on both sides of the Channel. Mr. Spectator's friend Leonora was not the only one, probably, whose copy of *Clélie* might open of itself to a scene of lovers in a bower. The long story of the French Lindamira is, to indulge in understatement, unlike that of our young woman. As for Scudéry's Cleodora (*Artamenes,* Part V, Book III), she reminds us of Lindamira's rival only in living with aunts. In the case of Doralisa there is something more; in her lively humor and wit attended by goodness and sweetness of disposition, in her unusual beauty and even in her age she seems to have been a copy of Doralisa, the entertaining friend of the Princess Panthea (*Artamenes,* Part V, Book I) whom Dorothy Osborne in a letter written in 1653 commended for her ideas on the choice of a husband.

But in spite of all its variety of indebtedness to the French romances — I have not mentioned the inserted letters and the portraits — *Lindamira* is a different sort of work. A brief sketch of the other contributing influences will account for some of the difference.

Writers in England who had adopted the personal letter as a fictitious narrative device had, more often than not in recent years, allied it with a humorous mood and a realistic, even risqué intention. Mrs. Manley's set of letters describing a coach journey from London to Exeter (1696), Charles Gildon's *Postboy Rob'd of his Mail* (1692), and the anecdotal letters that Brown himself had been issuing illustrate the tendency. Though the basic design of *Lindamira* has little in common with the schemes of these pieces, they may have aided the author in creating an impression of "the natural temper of the inhabitants of this our island."

Restoration drama must be considered, too. That Thomas Shadwell's satiric comedy *The Virtuoso* (1676) contributed to the humorous characterization we would assume on the basis of Lindamira's remarks about the foolish old suitor she calls Sir Formal Trifle. Really, the old man resembles Shadwell's Sir Samuel Hearty as well as Sir Formal. Lindamira's treatment of the old beau and of young Philander and later her bad manners toward Xantippe remind one, furthermore, of the conduct of the forward young ladies, Clarinda and Miranda, in *The Virtuoso*. The author of our book, like Lindamira herself, must have attended the playhouse more than once. English humor and heartiness and common sense have served to coach and restrain the author in her imitation of what she liked in the *roman*.

For it is the social attitude and the moral tone of *Lindamira* as much as the story and form that make the work notable. There is an innocence of mind in our narrator, an ethical standard for herself and others that quite separate her book from the popular *Five Love-letters from a Nun to a Cavalier* and the fiction of Mrs. Behn and Mrs. Manley. Mme. de Scudéry may be partly responsible, but the art of *Lindamira* is such as to make the heroine seem real, English, and her virtue her own. Her moralistic propensities on the one hand and her occasional crudity of manners on the other strengthen this impression. But that a woman's literacy and judgment were not expected to be as great as her virtue appears plainly more than once in the narrative.

Everyone knows the faults of the middle-class mind — its deplorable inability to find a graceful answer to the question of pleasure and decency, its mysterious preference for security rather than originality and intensity, its incorrigible social ambition and love of the details of high life, its luxuriating in sentiment while it keeps its eye on the dry article money, its gaucherie and its addiction to romance. All these characteristics, with whatever of criminality they may seem to possess, appear in *Lindamira*. The excursion, by way of a fortunate and improbable cousin, into the society of Fontainebleau in the Third Part accentuates not only the angle of inclination of the bourgeois social gaze but also the dissimilar quality of the society that Lindamira frequented.

The prefatory title, "The Lover's Secretary," which Wellington used for the second edition of the book (1713) might mislead some people, especially those who were thinking of a volume of French "Billets Doux, Letters Amorous, Letters Tender" published in 1692 as *The Lover's Secretary,* into expecting something passionate and affected. Yet a number of recent "Secretary" books teaching manners, propriety, and epistolography to decent citizens would guide the majority in the right direction. There was a public waiting for *Lindamira.* A fine view of it can be had in the diary kept by a serious young gentleman of the Middle Temple named Dudley Ryder. On Saturday, May 31, 1716, sitting on a river bank near Hackney with the young ladies of his aunt's household, Ryder heard talk about *Lindamira* and love. On Sunday he and Cousin John read and discussed a sermon by Archbishop Tillotson and then analyzed the impropriety of an established church. On Monday, besides calling on a dying friend, he looked into *Lindamira* for the first time. There are in it, he finds, "a great many very natural thoughts and turns of humor and passion which I am well pleased with" (*The Diary of Dudley Ryder 1715-1716,* transcribed by William Matthews, London, 1939, pages 209-11).

As *The Adventures of Lindamira* was a pioneering effort drawing on two kinds of literature, we need not be surprised to discover that the style is somewhat unsteady. Part of the trouble is, no doubt, that Brown did not revise and correct the manuscript of the lady of quality with equal thoroughness throughout. Hence the first eleven letters are more jaunty in mood and more facetious in manner than the rest, and the Doralisa section, composed appropriately in an elevated style approximating that of the French romances, he seems not to have modified at all. Lindamira had not the benefit of any *Spectator* papers lying on her boudoir table to teach her a style uniformly familiar but not coarse, uniformly elegant but not ostentatious. And Tom Brown, who less needed Addison's help, wisely did not eliminate either the "natural softness" or the revealing stiltedness of the lady's pen.

Some of the priggishness of both spirit and expression may be due to the technical difficulty of presenting such a heroine and such a story through the report of the young lady herself. The epistolary technique, as we see, has its disadvantages in addition to its appealing virtues. The management of the letter form is no more realistic here than in Richardson's novels. Lindamira's powers of recall in narrative, if surprising, are not the fantastic sort with which Mme. de Scudéry endowed Meleagenes and Celeres. One could say, too, in defense of the construction of the book that the digressive narratives dealing with Doralisa and with Octavius were inserted to fill empty intervals of time in Lindamira's history. And if the reversals and complications come in the Fourth Part with unfamiliar speed, the practice of contemporary playwrights, not to mention later novelists, should palliate her offense.

Of whom are we speaking? Who wrote *Lindamira*? It seems impossible to say. That it was not, in the first place, Thomas Brown I am convinced, as I have elsewhere made clear.* Brown habitually wrote fluently, and in the many original and translated letters which he published, the flexibility and naturalness of expression are conspicuous. Even had he set out to do so, it is doubtful whether he could have achieved the stiffness of Lindamira's unpracticed pen. Actually, too,

* Benjamin Boyce, *Tom Brown of Facetious Memory* (Cambridge: Harvard University Press, 1939), pp. 103–8.

such a picture of feminine conduct and feminine feeling as her letters provide was beyond him: it is too decent, too delicate, too girlish for him to have invented. A little reading in almost any of his works would convince most readers of this truth; a mere glance at his *Marriage Ceremonies; as now Used in all Parts of the World* (1704) would take care of the rest. Probably the author was not a man at all. That the work was a translation by Brown is also improbable. His methods in such work — and he was one of the most successful translators in that day of translations — varied according to the text and his mood, but it is hard to believe that the liberties he took with Voiture and Scarron and Mme. de Pringy's *Differens Caracteres des Femmes du Siecle* (issued as *A Legacy for the Ladies* in 1705) would not sooner or later have appeared here if the whole manuscript were his. When Brown and his publishers used the phrase "revised and corrected" they seem ordinarily to have meant exactly what the words imply.

It is possible that the original of *Lindamira* was a French work and that Wellington gave Brown someone else's translation of it to edit. There are one or two oddities of syntax in the book which might be accounted for as the result of poor translating. In that case, whether it was Brown or his predecessor who supplied the local color and skillfully wove in the material from *The Virtuoso* remains an awkward question. Brown knew the play, but that circumstance hardly settles the question. Humor seems to have been part of the original design; Brown probably added to it. Certainly his characteristic farcical touch can be seen in some of the language.

The likeliest hypothesis is that an Englishwoman, well read in Scudéry and familiar with *The Virtuoso,* wrote the whole story of Lindamira, inserting in it the Doralisa digression either as a successful imitation of *précieux* matter and style or as her own translation of something in French. Brown would then be responsible, as announced, only for surface revisions. Whatever the explanation, it is ironic that the English book most nearly prophetic of Richardson's novels and the most appealing middle-class heroine in English fiction before Pamela and Sophia Western and Clarissa should have gone into the world under the sponsorship of that soiled Tory wit and haunter of taverns, Tom Brown.

Bibliographical Note

The Adventures of Lindamira, A Lady of Quality. Written by her own hand, to her Friend in the Country. In IV. Parts. Revised and Corrected by Mr. Tho. Brown was first announced for sale in *The Post Man* on January 10, 1702. It came out as an octavo. In the Term Catalogues for Easter term, 1703 (Arber's edition, III, 347), Richard Wellington, the original publisher, announced a printing of *Lindamira* in "Twelves," but I find no record otherwise of such an edition. On October 22, 1712, *The Spectator* announced the publication "This Day" of "The Lovers Secretary, or, The Adventures of Lindamira, a Lady of Quality, giving an Account of her Amours and Intreagues from Fifteen Years to Fifty. Pr. 2s.6d." The same advertisement ran three more times before Wellington caught up with himself and, on November 28 and 29, deleted the unfortunate last five words. The book, a duodecimo called *The Lover's Secretary: or, The Adventures of Lindamira, A Lady of Quality. Written to her Friend in the Country. In XXIV Letters. Revis'd and Corrected by Mr. Tho. Brown. The Second Edition* (London: Printed for R. Wellington), bore the date 1713 in its title page. (Conceivably it was made up of sheets printed in 1703.) In this edition, several copies of which survive, many of the typographical errors of the first edition were corrected, but the text, except for a few unimportant rewordings of two or three sentences in Letters XXIII and XXV, remained substantially the same.

A "Third Edition," duodecimo, appeared in 1734. A "Fifth Edition," in sixes, was issued in Dublin in 1745 by Margaret Rhames, who in 1751 issued the book again, now as an octavo, with a title page not specifying the number of the edition. An error in the first edition of miscounting the eighteenth letter as the seventeenth caused the printer to announce in the title page that the volume contained twenty-four letters whereas actually there were twenty-five. The title pages of the later editions preserved the error.

The text of the present edition is based on that of the possibly unique copy of the first edition belonging to the University of Minnesota Library. The error in numbering the letters has been corrected, and the text of a missing leaf (sig. D 4) has been supplied from a copy of the second edition belonging to the Yale University Library (from "During the time of this diversion," page 30, to "which were in these terms," page 31). In order to enable the modern reader to meet *Lindamira* on the same terms of easy acquaintance which have ordinarily characterized his first meeting with *Moll Flanders* and *Tom Jones* I have modernized spelling and punctuation and have occasionally modified the paragraphing. Although a number of emendations, listed on page 167, appeared desirable, I have tried, in imitation of the first editor, to preserve colloquial phrases and extraordinary grammatical constructions lest I damage the "natural softness" of Lindamira's pen.

Finally, the reader need not be surprised to learn that still another lady has been involved in the adventures of *Lindamira* —the editor's wife, whose contribution of aid and advice should not go unrecorded.

B. B.

Books

PRINTED FOR R. WELLINGTON, AT THE DOLPHIN AND CROWN AT THE WEST END OF ST. PAUL'S CHURCHYARD

Five Love Letters from a Nun to a Cavalier; done out of French into English; by Sir Roger L'Estrange. The second edition, with the Cavalier's Answer.

De Re Poetica, or Remarks upon Poetry, with Characters and Censures of the Most Considerable Poets, whether Ancient or Modern, Extracted out of the Best and Choicest Critics; by Sir Thomas Pope Blount.

Sir Thomas Blount's Essays on Several Subjects; the third impression, with very large additions; besides a new Essay of Religion, and an Alphabetical Index to the whole.

Of Education, especially of young gentlemen, in two parts. The sixth edition enlarged.

Cinque Letters D'Amour D'une Religieuse Portuguise, Ecrites au Chevalier de C. Officier Francois en Portugal, Derniere Edition. Translated into English by Sir Roger L'Estrange: the English being on the opposite page for the benefit of the ingenious of other languages.

All the histories and novels written by the late ingenious Mrs. Behn, in two volumes in 8vo., each volume 5s.

A Natural History of the Passions; by Walter Charlton, M.D. The second edition enlarged.

Familiar Letters, in two parts; written by the Right Honourable John late Earl of Rochester, to the Honourable Henry Savil, Esq.; and other letters by persons of honour and quality, with letters written by the most ingenious Mr. Thomas Otway, and Mrs. K. Philips. Published from their original copies, with modern letters, by Thomas Cheek Esq., Mr. Dennis, and Mr. Brown. The second edition with additions.

The Elements of History from the Creation of the World, to the Reign of Constantine the Great, containing the history of the monarchs, in a new order and method, together with a view of the contemporary kingdoms, and commonwealths; and a brief account of their magistracies, and politic constitutions, done for the use of young students; by William Howel, LL.D. Translated from the Latin.

Scarron's novels, *viz*. The Fruitless Precaution. The Hypocrite. The Innocent Adultery. The Judge in His Own Cause. The Rival Brothers. The Invisible Mistress. The Chastisement of Avarice. The Unexpected Choice. Done into English with additions; by J. D. Esq.; The fourth edition corrected.

Five new plays, *viz*. The Surprisal, Committee, comedies; and The Indian Queen, Vestal Virgins, Duke of Lerma, tragedies; as they are acted by His Majesty's Servants, at the Theatre Royal, written by the Honourable Sir Robert Howard. The second edition, corrected.

A collection of novels, in two volumes in 8vo. *viz*. The Secret History of the Earl of Essex and Queen Elizabeth. The Happy Slave. The Double Cuckold. The Art of Pleasing in Conversation, by Cardinal Richelieu.

Heroine Musketeer, or Female Warrior, in four parts. Incognita, or Love and Duty Reconciled; by Mr. Congreve. The Pilgrim, in two parts.

A New and Easy Method to Understand the Roman History, with an exact chronology of the reign of the emperors; an account of the most eminent authors, when they flourished; and an abridgment of the Roman antiquities and customs, by way of dialogue, for the use of the Duke of Burgundy: done out of French, with very large additions and amendment; by Mr. Thomas Brown.

Dryden's plays in 2 vol. Lee's plays 1 vol. Otway's plays 1 vol. Shakspear's plays 1 vol. Congreve's works 1 vol. Wycherly's plays 1 vol. Behn's plays 2 vol. 8vo. Also gentry may pick novels stitched, at six shillings a dozen, and be furnished with all sorts of plays.

THE
ADVENTURES
O F
LINDAMIRA,
A Lady of Quality.

Written by her own hand, to
her Friend in the Country.

In IV. Parts.

Revised and Corrected by
Mr. *Tho.* Brown

London, Printed for *Richard Wellington,*
at the *Dolphin* and *Crown in* St. *Paul's*
Church-yard. 1702.

The Preface

'Tis needless to make out the usefulness of performances of this nature. Though amorous intrigues are commonly charged with vanity and folly, yet when they are calculated according to the measures of virtue and decency, they are equally instructive and diverting. To expose vice and disappoint vanity, to reward virtue and crown constancy with success, is no disserviceable aim. All virtuous readers must needs be pleased to see the virtuous and constant Lindamira carried with success through a sea of misfortunes, and at last married up to her wishes; not to mention the strokes of wit, the agreeable and innocent turns, and the just characters of men and things that drop from her artless pen.

If the histories of foreign amours and scenes laid beyond the seas, where unknown customs bear the greatest figure, have met with the approbation of English readers, 'tis presumed that domestic intrigues, managed according to the humours of the town and the natural temper of the inhabitants of this our island, will be at least equally grateful. But above all, the weight of truth and the importance of real matter of fact ought to overbalance the feigned adventures of a fabulous knight-errantry.

We have taken care to correct the style where the rules of grammar and the humour of the English language required an alteration, but so as not to disguise the natural passion or to depart from the natural softness of the female pen.

Letter I

Believe me, this is the greatest proof I can give of my sincere friendship to my dear Indamora, that I comply with her in a request so disagreeable to my own inclinations as to make her a narrative of my adventures, being so unfit to pen a history, although my own. But if you can excuse the inaccuracies of my language, as things offer themselves to my thoughts I will impart them to my dearest friend, in whose discretion I so much confide as to be sure she will not expose my follies; and since her goodness has made her so much embrace my interest as to give herself the trouble to be better informed of the particulars of my life, I ought not to deny her so small a satisfaction; and I am fully persuaded she has indulgence enough to excuse the indiscretion of my youth, therefore shall not scruple to advertise her of the most secret thoughts and movements of my heart.

I shall pass over those little occurrences of my life till I arrived to my sixteenth year, during which time nothing remarkable happened unto me. I was then blessed in a good mother, who never failed me, to give me all the necessary instructions of virtue and honour, and after what manner I ought to comport myself in all companies; ever telling me that pride in young women was as injurious to their fortune as an easy believing temper might prove on the other hand, and whatever addresses might be made to me, that I should give no encouragement till I had first acquainted her with them. The great esteem I had for my mother, and the high opinion I had of her virtue, and the extraordinary affection she ever expressed for me extorted from me this promise, that I would always be governed by her advice and that my will should center in hers. But at the same time I made my request she would not force my inclinations out of any consideration of estate or interest of alliance, and I gave her this solemn promise, never to marry without her consent and approbation. My mother, being well satisfied in what I promised her, as freely granted my request; and this reciprocal promise having passed between us, my mother was very easy in her thoughts about me, and the affection she had for me made her conceive a very advantageous opinion of my conduct, which eased her of those fears that usually attend a mistrustful temper in mothers, that their children must be guilty of great indiscretions if out of their sight; but on the contrary she never debarred me of the liberty of seeing such friends as were most agreeable to my own temper.

As for public diversions I never was much addicted to 'em, and that which confirmed me in this humour was for the sake of two young ladies of fortune, of indifferent beauty but very genteel and sparkish, who were of a humour to be at all public places of rendezvous, as plays, balls, music-meetings, Hyde Park, St. James's and Spring Garden. One day, being at a friend's house who had a young daughter near my own age in whose conversation I took much delight, I went thither to spend my afternoon, taking with me a new piece of work wherein I wanted her ingenious fancy to assist me in the contrivance. Whilst I was there, came in two very beauish sparks to visit my dear companion Valeria (for so was she called). They entertained us with the news of the town and of the last comedy, and pleasantly reproached us for being at home when all the fine ladies of beauty and quality were at the play. As for my own part, I told 'em I took more pleasure in looking on my work than others did in beholding all the pageantry of the operas. To this one of 'em replied (whose name was Mr. W——) that 'twas pity we were not of the humour of the two ladies I have already mentioned, that were at the play almost every day. "The devil take 'em," says t'other, "all places are filled with their ugly faces. I'd as live see a toad as their two long noses appear." To this Valeria replied that if she and I were of the same humour, he would say as much of us. But Mr. S—— excused himself for using so coarse an expression, and to atone for his crime he told us both very obligingly that our faces would command an universal respect, and that the critics in beauty would go with pleasure to those places where they could delight their eyes in beholding two such miracles of nature. The large encomiums he made on this occasion I ascribed to the merits of Valeria and the too well-grounded admiration he had of her beauty, for she was certainly a person infinitely charming.

And to deal sincerely with you, Indamora, that afternoon's conversation was the occasion that I resolved with Valeria not to be seen in public places, and that our faces should give as little offence as possible. We concluded upon this expedient, not to go often to our own parish church but change our place as often as the week came about. This humour we pursued a good while. For my mother not being very well, she kept her chamber for two or three months, for she, knowing I was in Valeria's company, remained very well satisfied, so that I had the opportunity of gratifying my own foolish humour; but after we had continued our rambling fancies for some time, an accident befell me for a punishment of my folly.

It happened one Sunday we went to Whitehall chapel, where I observed a gentleman had his eyes perpetually fixed on me, and whenever I looked that way, I found him still in the same posture; this I must confess put me extremely out of countenance, so that I was forced to rise up in my own defence and turn away my head. The confusion I was in made me give

7

little attention to what the minister said, whom I thought very tedious. But at last there was a general release, and Valeria and myself were the first that made an attempt to go out, the crowd being so great we could not without much difficulty disengage ourselves; but when I was at liberty and that I could breathe the fresh air, I turned about to Valeria to tell her I never was in so much confusion as at the spark that ogled me, whom it seems she had observed as much as myself. "I doubt not," said she, "but you have made a conquest of that beau, for I dare swear for him he was more intent on you than the minister that preached. Now is your time, Lindamira," continued she, "to do full execution with your eyes, and I hope you'll use your victory with moderation." She rallied me exceedingly for being so concerned for being looked on, and as we were on our way home I observed an ordinary man that pulled off his hat to me; and without looking him in the face I returned his civility, but Valeria knew him to be a porter I used to employ upon business, and as by accident she turned her head she perceived the spark a-talking to this fellow and told me of it, which extremely vexed me, for I concluded this ignorant blockhead would not have the sense to evade any questions that might be asked by Philander (for that is the name I gave him) and that he would certainly know by his means who I was.

Valeria did so unmercifully tease me that I could hardly pardon her raillery, which she continued till we got home, at which place I think most convenient to take leave of you and to give you some respite after so long and so ill-penned a narrative. But let the acknowledgments I have made of my disabilities plead for me, for nothing but your absolute commands could prevail with me to give, under my own hand, how indiscreetly I have governed myself. But am in all sincerity, my dearest Indamora,

Your most faithful friend and servant,
Lindamira

Letter II

MY DEAREST INDAMORA,

About two days after, my maid (whom Valeria called by the name of Iris) brought me a letter which the said Roger the porter gave her; though I knew not the hand, I opened it, and soon perceived it came from a lover, though unknown to me. The natural curiosity that attends our sex prevailed with me to read it, and though I have not the letter by me, to the best of my remembrance it was to this effect: that he was become the most amorous of men since he saw me, and was not able to drive my fair idea out of his mind; he begged I would permit him to wait on me, that he might tell me with his own mouth how great an admirer he was of me, and much to this purpose.

I sent for Roger, demanding of him from whom he had the letter and from what place. He told me, from a brave gentleman of the Temple. I inquired his name, which he readily told me, adding that he was a very familiar obliging gentleman and had a notable headpiece of his own; and as I knew Roger was none of the best judges of a man's sense and breeding, I had not a better opinion of Philander for the character he gave him. When he had answered all my questions, I bade him return this answer to the gentleman: that had I known from whence the letter came, I would have returned it to him if it had not been opened, and that I was highly displeased at his boldness, and absolutely forbade Roger bringing me any more letters. But before I dismissed him, I added one query more, which was, how he came to be employed by this gentleman, knowing that he plied a great way off from the Temple. He then told me that as I passed by, he putting off his hat to me that day we had been at the chapel, Philander, who had followed us, inquired of him my name and the place of my abode, to which questions he having answered, the gentleman commanded him the next morning to come and receive his orders.

In the afternoon Valeria, according to her usual custom, came to pass with me a few hours. I accosted her with the wonderful news I had to tell her concerning the letter I received from Philander. She laughed at me extremely, telling me I was rightly served for being so offended at his looks, but she hoped his letter had not given me so much offence. I recounted to her all the discourse I had with Roger, whom I had charged to bring me no more letters. "But have you forbid him bringing me any?" replied Valeria pleasantly, at the same time produced a letter from the same hand, and to prevent my asking how she came by it, she told me that Roger had brought it to her from a gentleman who was very ambitious of her acquaintance, but she might reasonably imagine it was for Lindamira's sake. I was very impatient to know what answer she returned; which was that she would not permit of his coming to wait on her, till she knew the sentiments of her friend, which she did believe would not encourage his visits without her mother's knowledge, and then she laid her commands upon the porter not to bring her any more letters.

I gave my dear Valeria a thousand thanks for the good office she had done me, believing this would blast all his hopes, and that I should be troubled no more with the importunity of a fluttering beau, whose genius only lies in dressing and saying amorous things. "But," said Valeria to me, "prithee tell me, my dear Lindamira, what sort of a man would be most agreeable to your humour? For Philander seems to be a person very deserving, he has a good presence and seems to have wit, and yet you hate him, only because he is become your admirer? What accomplishments must he or anyone have to render him worthy of your affections?" I told her it was not a delicate shape or a fine face that could charm me, but a person of a tender and generous soul, one that was not capable of a disingenious action to his friend, that was master of a sound and solid judgment, and had wit enough, but not too much, least he should discover my ignorance. "In fine," said I, "Valeria, I think that my happiness would consist in having an absolute empire over the heart of a virtuous person." "You have given so good a description of an accomplished person," replied Valeria, "that I wish it may be your fortune to reign absolute in the heart of such a one. But 'tis not usual to meet with those that can excite true love and admiration at the same time; and I fear," added she, "that you may keep your heart long enough, if you don't bestow it till you meet with one who is owner of all these perfections." In such sort of discourse we passed that afternoon, but I never thought the day long enough when I was in her company, such pleasure there is to converse with those one delights in. But Valeria was a person that was extremely pleasing, having abundance of wit and no affectation but much discretion, and I ever preferred the sweet enjoyment of her company before any diversions of the town. But since 'tis not her history I am to write, I will pursue my former narration, and acquaint you with the fopperies of Philander.

The Sunday following, after evening prayer, came the minister of the parish to wait on my mother, and Philander along with him. My mother sent for me into her chamber and bid me go and entertain Mr. G—— till she came. I obeyed her, but never was I more surprised than when I beheld Philander in the room. I was in dispute with myself if I should advance or retreat, but being obliged to be civil to Mr. G—— I acquitted myself as well as I could, and made my compliment to him.

Mr. G——, who was an ingenious man, wanted not for discourse to pass the time till my mother came, and then I was obliged to change my seat, and could not avoid setting by Philander, who all this time had not spoke one word, but sighed heartily whilst Mr. G—— entertained my mother (which seemed to be about business of consequence, for sometimes he spoke low). Philander took the opportunity to discover the weakness of his soul and his intolerable foppery; he was very loquacious, yet he often complained he wanted rhetoric to express his sentiments, which he did in such abominable, far-fetched metaphors, with incoherent fragments out of plays, novels, and romances, that I thought he had been really distracted. 'Tis impossible to represent to you the several grimaces, the gestures of his hands and head, and with what eagerness he plied his nose with snuff, as if that would have inspired his shallow noodle with expressions suitable to the occasion. I said all to him that my aversion could suggest, which I thought was enough to put a young lover out of hopes and frighten my parchment hero from making a second assault at my heart, which I was sure was proof against any impression he could make. But Philander was resolved to persist in tormenting me, and in a foppish impertinent way told me he would wait on me, whether I would or no, for he could not live without the sight of me. At length Mr. G—— took leave of my mother, and I was delivered from the conversation of one of the most ridiculous, fantastical fops the town ever bred.

When they were gone my mother asked me how I liked that gentleman. "As well, madam," said I, "as 'tis possible to be pleased with a conceited coxcomb, who has only a fair outside, but has neither sense nor brains to recommend him." "You are very satirical," said my mother, "for methinks he is a very pretty, well-bred gentleman." I told my mother that appearances were often fallacious, that I could discover no charms he had but the genteel toss with his wig and the grand slur that indeed was handsome enough, yet he was my aversion, for I could never have a true esteem for anyone so monstrously foppish. "But," replied my mother, "he has a good estate and is a counselor at the Temple and is very much taken with you, as Mr. G—— tells me, and in my opinion ought not to be slighted." But as my mother had promised not to force my inclinations, I did not apprehend much trouble from Mr. G——'s intercession on Philander's behalf, who made me a visit three or four days after and came in a dress suitable to his design, if fine clothes, well-chose and well put on, would have altered my opinion of him. My mother commanded me to go into the parlor to him, and to show some complacency to a gentleman that had an esteem for me. I obeyed my mother, but with all the reluctancy imaginable, which was easily discovered in my looks, and gave Philander some reason to fear that my heart was not so easy a prize as he imagined. After the first ceremonies, he asked me the cause of that chagrin that appeared in my eyes, and did hope that his presence did not contribute to it. I took the opportunity to assure him I was surprised to see him after the repulses I had given him, for I was not of the humour to encourage the affection of anyone only to add trophies to my victories, and that I thought it more for reputation to have no lovers at all, than such as I could have no esteem for. "Then, madam," said he, "I perceive I am not of that number that are blessed with your esteem or friendship," and retreating back a step or two as if he had been thunderstruck, he cursed his stars for loving one (as he said) so fair, and yet so cruel; and sighing said, "When I reflect on the severity of my destiny and what despair you drive me to, I am of all men the most unhappy; but could I represent to you the torments of love, the hopes, the fears, the jealousies that attend a violent passion, it would certainly work upon your generous humour and would prevent those miseries that accompanies a despairing lover." I harkened to his harangue without interrupting him, and when he had squeezed out his last sentence, I took upon me to represent the unhappiness of a precipitate inclination, and that the effects of it were nothing but sighs and a fruitless repentance, and however refined his passion might be, I had not so much good nature as to favour it; and being not willing to give way to the freedom of those thoughts I had of his foppery, I resolved to consider him as he was, and to treat him with respect, and ingeniously to confess I had so great an indifferency for him that it was impossible for me to vanquish it, whatever violence I used upon my inclinations, and that if he was truly generous, he would not give himself the trouble of coming any more to me.

At these words the poor lover seemed much concerned, and struggling between love and generosity, he at last said that he would obey me and banish himself from my presence, for he did believe the sight of him was odious to me; and since I was so niggardly of my favours, his life would be filled with nothing but disasters, and out of my presence it would seem a dull insipid being, and added also that he would take a voyage at sea and travel for some time, in hopes that absence would work the effect I desired. I confirmed him in his pretended resolution, representing to him the advantages that young gentlemen received by traveling, that they might improve their stock of wit, their judgment, and whatever their genius led 'em to; and that in France love and gallantry was so much practiced and encouraged, that I believed he would be esteemed in the first rank of the most gallant men of Paris, since he knew so well how to admire our sex and to extol imperfections for excellencies, and that flattery was a bait so easily swallowed, that none would question his judgment.

Some more discourse we had upon this subject, wherein he accused me of too much cruelty, and that I was guilty of great tyranny that would see him languish in despair. But the pious resolution he had taken of traveling, I told him, would prevent my seeing an object that could raise no compassion in me. He then perceived I rallied him, and not being willing to be the subject of my contempt, he begged leave to take his last farewell of me. That pleasing sound so charmed my ears, that I was ready to receive his salute before he was rose from his chair, which confirmed him more in the opinion of my aversion to him. And according to the ancient dialect of lovers, he blamed his fate and deplored his misfortune and then took his last adieu.

When he was gone I gave an account to my mother of what had passed. I believe my proceedings did not agree with her judgment, but she said little to me of it and thought me very difficult to please.

But, my Indamora, my time was not yet come that the little god of love took a revenge for my insensibility. My next tormentor was an old, stiff, ceremonious knight, to whom I gave the name of Sir Formal Trifle. But having spun out this letter too long already, I shall defer the recital of his addresses till the next opportunity I have of conveying my thoughts to my dear friend, with whom I wish myself daily, and that I could make you a visit in your charming solitude, which you have so ingeniously described, that I long to partake of your pleasure in your solitary walk of high elms, which brings into my remembrance some passages of my life which you shall be acquainted with in the sequel of my story. Farewell, my dear Indamora. I am,

Your Lindamira

Letter III

I shall, my dearest Indamora, succinctly run over the accident that brought me acquainted with Sir Formal Trifle, that I may the sooner come to that part of my story that has occasioned the curiosity of the cause of that great misfortune that has cost me so many sighs and tears.

And I think two months had scarce passed over after Philander had left me at liberty, but my mother and myself were invited to dinner by an uncle of Valeria's, where was to be only a select number of friends; and knowing Valeria would be there, I went with more pleasure than I should have otherwise gone, if my pleasant companion had not been one of the number. At dinner, according to custom, all the ladies' healths were drank, and at last it came to my turn; and as the fates would have it, it fell to Sir Formal's lot to begin it. "Madam," said he, "my fair opposite, 'tis ordained by the stars above that I should be that happy man that has the honour (though undeservedly) to begin the most amiable Lindamira's health." This long harangue was so surprising to me and so uncommon that if I had not been under some restrictions I should have discovered my ill-breeding by laughing in his face. But this dignified fop, for fear I did not apprehend his compliment, repeated the same words again, that he might have more efficacy upon my mind, and obliged all the gentlemen to follow his example. Now that you may know him the better, I will send you his portraiture drawn in as lively colours as ever Titian or Tintoret represented anyone to the life.

This knight was about the age of forty-five, tall, lean, and ill-shaped, but I could not discover the least relics of a good face. He was slow of speech, mightily opinionated of his own wit, one who delighted in hard words, and admired himself for his discourses, his fustian way of expressing his wretched thoughts (which he was pleased to misname oratory) and eloquence. At the same time he was insupportably impertinent in all companies. He would be giving his advice when he was never asked; and, to the mortification of all that conversed with him, he had a prodigious long memory, which made him never to omit the least circumstance that served to enlarge his story, so that all his auditors stood in need of what patience they had to support 'em under the fatigue (if I may so express it) of being obliged to give attention to him. Thus, my Indamora, have I given you a most exact description of this Sir Formal, without either magnifying or detracting from his merits.

As soon as dinner was over, Valeria and I withdrew from the company and went into a closet, where we had our fill of laughing; for all dinnertime he threw his eyes about as if he would have thrown 'em at me, and sent me so many amorous glances and made so many wry faces, that one would have imagined convulsion fits had seized him. I was particular in my inquiry whether he was bachelor or married man; if the latter, I had good nature enough to pity his lady, but if the former, I rejoiced to think that no woman was so unhappy to be subject to his humours, which to me seemed insupportable, especially the everlasting penance of hearing his impertinencies. "But," said Valeria, "what if the knight should become your lover, how would you receive him? For I am of opinion you have made a conquest of his heart already, and he never makes his application but to young ladies." "Is it possible," said I, "that he should have confidence to make love with that forbidding face?" " 'Tis most certainly true," replied Valeria, "and you need not doubt but he will make you a visit, which will last you six long hours by the clock. His discourse you'll find worse than his namesake's in *The Virtuoso*; he'll perpetually tease you with long narrations of his intrigues with young ladies, of favours received, of his compendious way of storming of hearts, and the insensibility of his own, for he pretends 'tis his greatest diversion to draw the fair sex into his snares." When Valeria had done speaking, I could not help admiring that anything that went on two legs and pretends to reason could be so vain, so conceited, and so abandoned to folly. The character she gave of him made me entertain a mortal aversion for him, and I heartily wished I might never see the face of him more.

But for the punishment of my sins, no question, Valeria and myself were called down to the dining room, and the first object I cast my eyes upon was Sir Formal, who came smirking towards me and offered me his hand to lead me to the other end of the room, which I could not civilly refuse him. He then began a long harangue upon the second chapter, as he expressed himself, of my incomparable perfections. "Madam," said he, "have you not heard of the robbery that was committed within these few hours at noonday? The party that was robbed lost his best jewel in his cabinet, and," continued he, "the pretty thief that stole the prize is within earshot of me." I could not comprehend his meaning, as being utterly unacquainted with his figurative way of speaking, and innocently told him I was altogether ignorant of the strange news he told me, and that I did not know how I ought to apply his simile. "To yourself," said he, "for you are the thief above-mentioned, and 'tis my heart that is lost," and so with this threadbare, fulsome, weather-beaten simile he persecuted me at least an hour, telling me that when he met with ladies of wit he chose to entertain them with allegories. What I have related to you was not so soon spoke as you may have read it over, for he drew out every syllable with as much grace as the slowest Spaniard in Castile, and this so effectually tired me that, like Prince Pretty-man in *The Rehearsal,* I was ready to fall asleep. But my mother released me from his tiresome conversation by telling me it was time to be gone, because she designed to make a visit to a friend before she went home.

I leave you to judge, my dear Indamora, of the joy I felt in my soul when I was summoned to be gone, for though I made a thousand little excuses, yet all this while I was not able to disengage myself from his company. When we were arrived at this place I made my complaint to a young lady of what penance I had undergone for an hour and related to her all the discourse, and she frankly told me that the condition I was in would rather provoke compassion than envy; but she reserved her pity for the future, for she foresaw my unhappiness would not end presently; for Sir Formal, according to his method having given me a taste of his wit, would certainly pursue me with his favours. I took this presage of the lady's for an ill-omen, and as I had already received the true marks of the beast from Valeria, it possessed me with so invincible a hatred to his person, that I believe all the persuasions in the world could not prevail with me to be civil to him if he came to visit me, which he failed not of doing in two days after. It happened to my great consolation that Valeria was with me when he came into the room; he saluted us both with his usual parade of ceremonies, and applauded us for our ingenuity and great wisdom in employing ourselves in work, for, saith he, "it diverts young ladies from thinking on the town intrigues, which so much corrupts the youth of our age; and my advice is, ladies," said he, "to continue in this method you have so happily begun." This methodical old coxcomb, that always went as regular as a pendulum, I imagined all the world either were or ought to be of his unpleasant humour; but he was much mistaken in us, for though we never pleaded for a criminal liberty, we hated form and slavish observations of old customs, and what our inclination led us to, that we generally gratified ourselves in.

But to return to Sir Formal, who failed not of making his character good, he made love to me in a manner quite different from other men, for he much enlarged on his own virtues, merits, and upon the conquests he had made, and mightily extolled his good humour and moderation, giving us to understand he was a great philosopher, had studied self-denial the most of any man. I heard him with much patience, for the knight being taken up wholly with his own good qualities, I found I had nothing more to do than to hearken to him, and this first visit was the only diverting one I ever had from him, for his entertainment was absolutely new. My mother was gone abroad when he first came in, but his visits being of the usual longitude of six hours, he was not gone before she returned home. He no sooner saw her but began a long-winded discourse of his own excellencies, and after he had entertained her thus for some time, he asked my mother if she had no design to marry her daughter, saying that he knew a man of quality and of a great estate, without incumbrances, was fallen desperately in love with her.

My mother replied that, I being very young, she had no thoughts of disposing of me yet; and besides, so few were happy in that case that she could not persuade me to alter my condition, for the observation she had made (by the sad experience of some of her friends) that few men loved their wives so well as their mistresses, and that marriage quite altered the constitution of their souls, and as saintlike, complaisant, and obliging as they appeared during their courtship, they became tyrants instead of husbands, and did so ill-use their power that they treated their wives like slaves, and had not that tenderness and affection for 'em as might be justly expected.

Sir Formal thought my mother entertained too severe an opinion of the ill-treatments of men to their wives, and did assure her that this person he mentioned had thoughts too tender and generous to use a wife like a slave, and, to be short, gave her to understand, that himself was the individual person that would render me happy. But my mother's sentiments were so conformable to my own, that she gave him no encouragement to hope that his love would be agreeable to my inclinations. At last he took his leave with these comfortable words, that he would often wait on me.

Sir Formal, to show himself a man of his word, came often indeed to see me, though he was as often told I was not at home or had company with me. But his success was the same, for my aversion increased by his continual importunity of persuading me to marriage; the very thoughts was enough to make me swound, and his fulsome letters completed my hatred; for never was so soft a passion as love so ill-expressed as what came from the pen of Sir Formal. This mortification continued at least three months, notwithstanding the frequent denials he had both from my mother and myself. But one day it came into my mind to put a trick upon him, for he had often told me that ladies of the best quality were in love with him, and that every day he received billet-doux from 'em, but slighted their kindness for my sake. I had no sooner contrived a way how to fathom him and try how real his love was to me, but I went to Valeria and acquainted her with my design, who was so kind as to approve of it, saying he deserved to be used scurvily, though she made some few objections at first for fear we should injure our own reputation in it; but I alleged so many reasons and so well satisfied her that we ran no hazard in this matter, that I brought my friend to comply with me.

I have not leisure to continue my narration, by reason of some business that obliges me to go out; but if Indamora is not surfeited with the recital of Sir Formal's amour, I can assure you I am, and shall make all the haste I can possible to disengage myself from so nauseous a subject. I am,

My dearest Indamora,

Your friend and servant,

Lindamira

Letter IV

Immediately I set myself to compose a letter, my dear Inda-mora, as from a lady much charmed with the eloquence of Sir Formal, who, being under some restrictions, could not find out a more convenient place for an hour's conversation than at the playhouse, therefore desired him to meet her there betimes in the pit before any company came, that she might have the more freedom of telling him the secrets of her soul. She described her clothes, which were rich and genteel, and yet was as great a snare to him as to any young flutt'ring beau in town. This letter I sent by a trusty messenger, that I was sure he received it, and did believe he would not fail a fair lady at the place of rendezvous.

In the afternoon I dressed up Iris in the same clothes I had described. This young girl had a great deal of wit, and therefore I thought her a fit person to banter the knight. Valeria and myself had dressed ourselves like women that had no design of making of conquests. This contrivance of ours we imparted to a gentleman that was related to me, in whose discretion I much confided. We all went in a coach to the play, but Iris and Mr. Z—— went out first, for he was to conduct her in and to sit behind her, as one that had no knowledge of her. He ordered the coach to drive to the door contrary to that Valeria and I came in at. When we were in the pit, there was only our own company, but in six minutes after, we see Sir

Formal Trifle enter. It was not difficult for him to imagine who was his fair captive, and to her he directed his steps and sets himself by her. Valeria and myself were at some convenient distance from 'em, so that we could not distinctly hear him, but by his gestures and vehemence we soon imagined his heart was caught; for he was deeply engaged in a very earnest discourse with her, and as she since related it to me, Sir Formal expressed himself very passionately to her, and importuned very earnestly to see her face, which she not granting, he pressed her more earnestly, and begged she would meet him at some other place where he might with more freedom tell her how much he was in love with her; "for of all the women I ever conversed with (which are of the best quality) I never was pleased with anyone's wit so much as yours, dear madam."

Iris returned his praises with great applauses of his merits, which had wrought this wonderful effect in her heart, and nothing but the difficulty of going out alone (for she was under the eye and guardianship of an old uncle) could prevent her giving herself the honour of his conversation another time. The old amoret was transported with these charming words and at her obligingness that in three nights she would meet at the place agreed upon, though she ran the hazard of her uncle's displeasure, but requested of him to leave her as soon as the play began. The joy he felt in his soul for this kind promise of the unknown lady was visible in his face, for he departed full of the thoughts of his being beloved, and consequently should be better treated than he was by me.

But whilst Iris was engaged with Sir Formal, Valeria and myself met with very good entertainment, for though we thought our ordinary dress would have secured us from any diversion of that sort, yet it was not our good fortune to escape so. To my lot there fell a spruce officer, who for an amusement exercised his wit in talking to one that little understood it. He said a thousand obliging things to persuade me he was charmed with me and believed I was not a person so mean as I appeared by my dress, for he was certain that under my mask there was much youth and beauty. I must confess that this sort of banter was not displeasing to me, though I had not vanity enough to believe I merited the praises he gave me; yet I was delighted with what he said, for he spoke his words with so good a grace, and there appeared so much good humour in his countenance, that I thought it was no crime to encourage the conversation of one who seemed so deserving. He asked me several questions about indifferent things which I had the good fortune to answer pertinently enough, and this confirmed him, he said, in the high opinion he had of my ingenuity. But since he had formed an idea of me in my mask that I was sensible did not belong to me, I thought it prudent not to convince him of his error, and though he used abundance of pretty arguments to let him see some part of my face, yet all his rhetoric was in vain. At length seeing he could not persuade me to gratify his request, when the play was almost done, "Madam," cries he, "you'll at least condescend to grant me one civil petition, and that is to suffer me to write to you." This request I thought more unreasonable than the other, for then I apprehended he must come to a further knowledge of me. I believe he partly guessed at my thoughts, and without giving me leave to explain myself he told me his letters should be left at any shop or place I thought fit, directed to anyone I pleased, and by what name I thought good, and he would give me a direction to write to him, and by this means we might hold a correspondence which would be extreme delightful on his side.

I do ingeniously confess to you, Indamora, that this proposition pleased me infinitely, for I was so much charmed with his conversation, that I formed in my mind no little pleasure from so agreeable a commerce. At last I resolved to grant his humble suit upon condition he would not follow me out of the playhouse nor ever make any inquiry who I was, if I did correspond with him; he promised an implicit obedience and, at my request, to be gone as soon as the play was done.

But 'tis time to say something of the adventure that Valeria had, whose fortune was not so good as mine; for the spark that applied himself to her was of a different humour from Colonel Harnando. His wit was abusive and full of detraction and the common scurrilous banter of pawning clothes for tobacco and brandy, which it seems is a science that some are great proficients in. She, not being used to that sort of discourse, was much offended at him, and her anger so improved his fancy that he run on at a most extravagant rate and ceased not tormenting her till the play began, and then he left her, as he said, to shift for herself.

As soon as the play was ended and the crowd pretty well dispersed, we went out, and Mr. Z——, who was our companion, took care of us and Iris, who had persuaded the knight to leave her as soon as the actors appeared on the stage. When we came home she gave us a full relation of the conquest her eyes had made, and how many amorous things this libidinous knight had said to her of his impatience of seeing her, which she had promised to grant in three nights, and that he had given a very advantageous character of himself, for it seems nothing would put him out of his old method. We had a great deal of laughing about him and, to carry on the jest farther, concluded Iris should send him a billet-doux to this purpose: that being informed since she last saw him that he courted a lady of a considerable fortune, whose youth and beauty far exceeded hers, she could not flatter herself so much as to think he would relinquish his pretensions for her sake, and she, not being of a humour to be content with part of his heart, chose rather to continue in that unhappy state she was in than be made more miserable by knowing she had so fair a rival; that to prevent a greater ill she would endeavour to withdraw her affections from him, believing it not possible for him to be guilty of an infidelity to the lady he loved; and she would conceal from him the little beauty that she has, lest he should quite repent him of the kindness he had for her in her mask, and therefore begged his pardon for the disappointment. In the postscript she told him that if he pleased to write, how he might direct to her. This letter I sent by the penny post the morning she was to meet him.

But the day after this adventure at the play, Sir Formal made his visit to me, and Valeria was there at the same time, for we were both full of expectation of having an account of his intrigue with the lady in the mask; and he failed not of recounting to us how much a young lady of quality was in love with him, and that she had writ to him to meet her at a friend's house (which he could not refuse) and that she expressed to him the most tender and passionate things in the world. "But for your sake, fair Lindamira," said he, "I have dashed all her hopes by telling her of the pre-engagement of my affection to a lady I should suddenly marry." Though I knew every syllable of this to be false, yet I had not patience to hear him when he talked of marriage, and I should rather have chose to have been shut up in some horrible vault with ghosts and hobgoblins, screech owls and bats, than to have been the bride of so nauseous and so disagreeable a man. At last I interrupted him, telling him that I thought I had never given him any ground to hope I would ever be his bride, or at least it was not my design to favour the deceit, and if the young lady could dissemble love so well as to persuade him into a belief so contrary to reason, he would do well to snap at her heart whilst she was in so good a humour to let him take it. And as there is no reason why some love blue, others red, green, or yellow, so 'twas not to be wondered that she should like what was my aversion. But Sir Formal could not bear the reproach of the lady's want of judgment, but said 'twas no contemptible thing to be Sir Formal Trifle's lady. "Then they that are fond of the title," said I, "you ought to honour with it."

But since I had conversed with Colonel Harnando, he seemed more insupportable to me than ever; and to pass away the time I called to Iris to bring us some coffee, for the clock had struck but four times since he came in. When it was brought to me, I could not but in civility offer him some, which he readily accepted, and being paralytic and the dish very full and the coffee scalding hot, he spilled it all upon his shins, which made 'em smart excessively. We could not help laughing at the unlucky accident, and ill nature prevailed so far that we knew not when to give over, which much enraged the knight, and put him out of humour. But at last I told him a remedy — to hold his shins to the fire, for one fire would drive out another, and it would be the best expedient he could use to persuade himself to love this young lady of quality to drive me out of his thoughts, for which I should be eternally obliged to him. But the anguish he was in put him in a fret, and in a great pet he left us before the six hours were expired. His absence always gave me great relief, for he still took care so to mortify me with his long, inconsistent speeches, that they were days of jubilee with me when he did not come.

As soon as he was gone, Valeria asked me if this was not the evening that I was to receive a letter from Colonel Harnando, which was then out of my thoughts, and I sent a messenger away immediately to the place assigned for the receiving of it, and with some impatiency waited the return of the messenger, believing the Colonel would have forfeited his word; but I found him to be one that was very punctual to his promise, which the quick return of him I sent confirmed me in when he presented me with this following letter.

COLONEL HARNANDO TO LINDAMIRA

Madam,

I am so far convinced that nothing can equal my fair unknown, that 'tis impossible for me to entertain any other notions of you than what are highly advantageous to your honour and reputation. Be kind, my charming fair, and deliver me out of this perplexity, that I may know on whom I have bestowed my heart and fixed my thoughts entirely. Were you but half so impatient to know your captive as I am to know my fair conqueror, you would, out of a sentiment of generosity, discover to me what I so ardently desire. You tell me, madam, that my letter shall be answered, which gives me some faint hopes that you will conceal yourself no longer from the knowledge of,

Madam,

Your most faithful admirer,
Harnando

I read this letter over several times, and though I was much pleased with the frolic, yet I could not harbour so mean an opinion of the Colonel's wit to believe he could have any affection for one that he had only seen in a mask; and as I would give him no occasion to reproach me with being worse than my word, I concluded upon sending him this answer, which Valeria approved to be enough to the purpose.

LINDAMIRA TO COLONEL HARNANDO

Sir,

I think myself extreme happy in the good opinion you have of me, and I should be infinitely to blame should I convince you of the error you are in, which is so much to my advantage that though I have youth (which I hope will extenuate my folly), yet the little beauty I have (should you see it) would oblige you to make vows against your passing your judgment on a mask for the future. You have by this artifice of writing prevailed with me to discover my ignorance to a person who is so good a judge of wit; and am liable to your censure, which pray let be as favourable as possible; and grant this petition to your friend and servant,

Incognito

I sent this answer by the penny post. What effects it produced you shall know in my next.

I am, my dear Indamora,
Your sincere friend and servant,
Lindamira

Letter V

Before I proceed any further concerning the Colonel, my
dearest Indamora, I must make a digression and give an account of the resentments of the knight, who left me that night
much dissatisfied with the treatment he received; and though
the accident was not intentionally on my side, yet he was
highly displeased that I laughed when I ought to have pitied
his misfortune; and being in great wrath with me, he returned
a very kind answer to the masked lady, which gave me much
diversion, as without difficulty you will imagine.

According to his custom he came to visit me. I was more
complaisant than ordinary, on purpose to bring about the discourse of the lady of quality. He told me, notwithstanding
the ill-usage he had received from me, that nothing could
shake his constancy; and though he had received a letter from
the lady, yet he would not give her another meeting (as she
desired) till he knew of a certainty, whether or no I would
vouchsafe him the blessing of being his co-partner in all his
worldly goods. I answered him, without any hesitation, that
to be his wife was to be of all women the most accursed, and
if he pleased he might let the lady know that I laid no claim
to his heart. Sir Formal received with indignation this answer,
for he had very high thoughts of his own merits, and told me
that his birth, person, and estate might challenge a kinder
treatment than what he received from me. To this purpose he

chattered a long time, but I returned him no answer; and to my relief there came some ladies to have me to Hyde Park, where I thought the air extreme refreshing, for his company and his tobacco together had almost tired me.

But when I returned at night I found a letter from the Colonel which was obliging, passionate, and kind; he used many arguments to persuade me into a belief that he was real in his pretensions and that I had a great ascendant over his heart, and was yet more impatient to see me than ever.

Though I was charmed with his wit, yet I received all he said as things that proceeded more from his exuberant brain than his heart and that these letters or the same expressions had been said to twenty women before me. However, I sent him an answer that gave him as little information who I was as my first did, and expressed as little desire to know him; but he might well enough see I was not displeased at the correspondence, which encouraged him to continue till such time as an accident broke it off.

During the time of this diversion I resolved the next time that Sir Formal came, to make him sensible that I knew him to be a vain, pragmatical, conceited coxcomb, and that I would confute him by his own letters, that he had not related one word of truth concerning his new mistress; and in order thereto, I gave directions to Iris what she should do when he came, for I made no scruple to affront one who had quite tired me out with his impertinencies.

When he came (which was not long first) I sent to Valeria to be witness of his looks and actions. After he had been with me an hour, Iris came hastily to me and brought me a letter, saying that a porter stayed for an answer, and out of a pretence of civility I asked Sir Formal's leave to read it before him, which he assented to. When I opened it, I found another enclosed and directed for Madam Price, which I seemed much to wonder at. When I had read my own, I read that, and giving it to Valeria, "See there, Valeria," said I, "how constant

Sir Formal is to me; this is he, that nothing could shake his constancy!" The knight seemed much amazed, but I believe he guessed he was betrayed, and asked me coldly why I reproached him with inconstancy? "I do not allege it as a crime to you, Sir Formal," said I, "for nothing can please me better than to find you what I ever wished you — that is, full of falsehood and disingenuity. But to prevent your excuse in this matter, I will read to Valeria the two letters.

MADAM,

I once thought myself happy in the entire affections of Sir Formal Trifle, who solemnly swore to me that he loved none but me; and when I was upon the point of resigning up my heart to him, I heard he is a pretender to yourself. Be so sincere, madam, as to let me know the truth, which if it be as fame reports, I will never see him more. I can only reproach myself with the too easy belief of the vows and asseverations that drew me into this snare. I am,

Madam, Your Servant

Whilst I read this letter, Valeria observed the uneasiness he was in, and would have prevented my reading the other, which were in these terms:

DEAR SOUL,

You injustly tax me with want of love, which is so great that I am in admiration of myself to find the magic there is in that passion, which has received an additional recruit by your jealousy of Madam R——, to whom I have no pretensions in the least; but as she is young and fair, I love to trifle away a few hours with her. But all my happiness centers in you, my lovely angel. Let nothing hinder me from enjoying your company, which is so ardently wished by, madam,

Your most obsequious, most humble servant, F. T.

I think I never saw a man look so like an ass as Sir Formal did, for he had not presence of mind to evade the thing by pretending his hand was counterfeited, or that it was a trick put upon him to try his sincerity. But his looks betrayed him; and being conscious of his fault, he made but slender excuses, and that eloquence he had so often boasted stood him in little stead; so that all he could say for himself, when I represented to him how unfaithfully he had related his intrigue with the lady and that nobody could confide in anything he said, was that he always spoke enigmatically, that it was his constant method, and if it was not grateful to my humour, he should not put himself out of his way to please the little pretenders of this age.

I seemed to resent the affront put upon me, that he came to see me only to trifle away a few hours, which he excused so foolishly that I plainly perceived that if he was put out of his road, he was the most empty, shallow monster in the universe.

After a long parley on both sides, Sir Formal took leave of me, saying it had been better for him had he never seen my face. I was not curious to pry into this mystery, but bade him heartily farewell, wishing him good success with the ladies of quality. The charming musical sound of his adieu filled my heart full of joy; but he only banished himself for six weeks, during which cessation I shall acquaint you with things more remarkable and more worthy of your knowledge.

You may remember, my dear Indamora, that in my first letter I mentioned one Mr. S—— who was an admirer of Valeria, whom you shall know by the name of Silvanus. This gentleman had a good estate equivalent to her fortune; he had many excellent qualities that served to recommend him to her affections; their loves were reciprocal, and in all human appearance they might live happy after marriage, for their humours were agreeable, and so was their age. After six months' courtship, Silvanus prevailed with Valeria to be married, and though she esteemed him very much (and indeed he was a person that merited all things), yet 'twas with much difficulty she consented to his proposals, for her liberty she preferred at a high rate; but at last the wedding day was appointed, and I had the honour to be one of her bride-maids. This marriage happened during the blessed truce I had from the importunity of Sir Formal. There was nothing remarkable at the wedding, which was consummated with much satisfaction to all her friends.

About a week after, Silvanus would have Valeria to the new play and me to accompany her thither. We both of us had the advantage of fine clothes and good dressing to set us off; but my dear Valeria had many advantages over me, for she was very lovely and full of charms, and the addition of fine jewels made her outshine persons of the greatest quality. Silvanus placed us in the king's box and went himself into the pit, but before the play was begun I discovered amongst the crowd Colonel Harnando. The sight of him gave me such a disturbance that I wished myself out of the house a thousand times. For Valeria being so gloriously dressed that she attracted the eyes of all the beaus in the pit, I setting next to her could not escape being looked upon, and being conscious of my own weakness, was afraid I should betray myself by my looks to be the person that corresponded with him. He fixed his eyes much upon me, which both pleased me and gave me great inquietudes; for so capricious is love, that I was uneasy if he looked on me, fearing he might dislike me, and then again I wished he might be pleased with me; but a sudden thought came into my mind that all women in general were pleasing to him, so that if he looked that way or turned his eyes another, I was dissatisfied with him, that all he could do would not please me. But I had this private satisfaction of seeing him that took up all my thoughts and of being seen by him, and yet he to be ignorant that I was there in view of him. He seemed that day more lovely than the first time I saw him, but whether it was that I sate more to the advantage of seeing him, or that the good opinion I had of him made me partial in my judgment, I voted him to be the handsomest in all the place, and I wished as much to know who he was as 'twas possible for him to know me; but my soul was full of prophetic fears that I was not the only woman he loved.

When I came home, I inquired of Silvanus who the Colonel was, whom I described by his clothes. He presently informed me that he was a man of quality, that he was lately married to a rich widow, and that they did not live very happily together; that he was a great professor of gallantry and a very amorous man. This news struck my heart like a thunderbolt, for then I knew I had more than a common esteem for him. 'Twas that time, my Indamora, that I stood in need of all my reason, prudence, and discretion, to hide from Silvanus the agitations of my soul. I reproached myself often for my indiscretion in believing what he said to me, which was in words so tender that they wrought a greater effect upon my heart than they ought. When I was alone with Valeria, I complained of my hard fate, that I should love a man not worthy of my affections because of his pre-engagement, and I could not without offence to my own honour and reputation continue my correspondence with him; so I took a full resolution to write to him but once more, to represent to him his crime and his folly, which I did the next night. What followed after I will acquaint you in my next. I am, my dearest Indamora, your

Most faithful, humble
servant, Lindamira

Letter VI

I must ingenuously confess to you, my dear Indamora, that I was sensibly afflicted at the discovery I made of the Colonel's infidelity, of whom I had conceived very high thoughts. I could not in all this time persuade myself to discover to him who I was, yet I was concerned that he should think that womankind were so easy of belief. But what can I say to extenuate my fault? I was young and unexperienced in the arts of love, and abandoned my thoughts too much in the contemplation of his merits. For Harnando had all the advantages of a fine education, and his person was charming, and that which pleased me most, I thought him neither fop nor beau. Several letters had passed between us which proved so pernicious to my repose; and I could not disguise my sentiments so well, but that he might plainly see I was not insensible of his affections. 'Tis needless to send you more than this one letter that I received the day after I had seen him at the play.

HARNANDO TO LINDAMIRA
I love too fondly not to be perplexed with deep despairs, since your obdurate heart will never yield to let me know who 'tis has robbed me of my repose. This is a misfortune not to be supported, for, my dearest love, my soul is so fondly fixed on you that I cannot bear a denial of what I so much wish. Your obliging concern for my indisposition has so linked my soul

to yours, that you can never doubt my kindness; ill-usage alone will make me smother what I feel. My dearest life, after what I have so often professed, you will deny me a sight of that face I believe so divinely fair; let me conjure you to heal the wounds you have given, and repent of your unkindness, and command my life.

Adieu

This letter wrought a contrary effect to all the former, for whereas those used to fill my heart full of joy, at the reading of this I was seized with a violent grief and shame, and confusion was seen diffused all over my face. I looked upon myself as a criminal, believing I might possibly have alienated his affections from his lady, who was a deserving person. I found I loved him, and represented to myself the danger in loving one already married, though all might be cloaked under the name of friendship; and fearing my opinion should alter, and knowing the imbecility of my nature as well as the power he had gained over my inclination, I sent him that night this letter.

LINDAMIRA TO COLONEL HARNANDO

Is it possible that after so many vows of an eternal fidelity, you can be guilty both of deceit and perjury? Though, alas, you deceived me, that adds not to your glory, and these mean achievements will not illustrate your trophies; and false vows and oaths will add much to your reputation! I was ignorant of the stratagems of love and judged of your sincerity by my own, which was incapable of a deceit or trick. What satisfaction could you propose in a reciprocal affection with me that had already plighted your faith in the presence of man and heaven? 'Tis in vain to deny that once I esteemed you, but you have taught me so much repentance, by misplacing my affections, that I may say I owe more to your crime than to my own reason for the cure of a passion that might have proved so pernicious to my reputation. But thanks to heaven, I am unknown to you, and shall forever let you remain in ignorance. Send me no more letters, for I have solemnly sworn never to answer them.

Adieu

You may perhaps wonder, my dear friend, at my fantastical humour in permitting Harnando to love me, and yet I concealed from his knowledge who I was. But I was so nicely scrupulous that I apprehended if once he knew me, it would lessen his esteem, and the manner of our acquaintance would make him harbour mean thoughts of me; and though it was the only frolic I was ever guilty of in that nature, yet I thought he would imagine it was my usual pastime. So ambitious was I of his good opinion, and though I sometimes half consented in my own thoughts to meet him at some friend's house, yet I was unalterable in my denials; and 'twas happy for me, for he had so engaging and obliging a way of expressing himself, that I should have abandoned my heart to the power of my destiny and not found it so easy a matter to have cured myself of a passion which on my side was grounded on virtue. I soon gained that victory over myself, that I may say he employed my thoughts but was a stranger to my heart.

I received several letters from him wherein he expostulated with me that souls being freeborn, they ought not to be enslaved by foolish customs, and if I had ever permitted him to have seen me, he would have acquainted me with his whole life and fortune. But I returned him no more answers, and being quite tired out with writing, he left off corresponding and, I believe, engaged himself in a new amour.

You have by the influence of your commands drawn from me a secret that none but my dear Valeria knew, of whose discretion I was so much assured, that to Silvanus I was confident she never spoke of it. But, my dear Indamora, one misfortune seldom comes alone, for I was now to lose my dear companion, who at her husband's request was preparing for the country, his relations having earnestly invited him, to congratulate with him his happiness with Valeria. I esteemed him as he was worthy in himself, but more as he was the husband of my dearest friend.

The news of her departure extremely afflicted me, for I had no friend in whom I could confide or that was capable of giving me advice like to herself. But before she went I was tormented with the returns of a love fit from Sir Formal, who was born to be a vexation to me, and that which added to my grief was, that 'twas never known he had been so constant to anyone as to myself, and 'twas believed he had a real passion for me, notwithstanding the ill-usage he received from me. But after the marriage of Valeria I was more abroad than ever I had been, for she telling me we were not like to enjoy one another long, she obliged me to be with her continually, and by this means I was often delivered from the fulsome love of one I hated. My mother, who was always very indulgent to me, and perceiving I grew melancholy, told me that if I had a mind, I should go to my grandmother's for two or three months, who had a pleasant and delightful seat in the country. She said to me, "Now that your friend is going out of town, it will no longer seem a place of pleasure to you." And also knowing it was the best way to get rid of Sir Formal (which nothing else would do), I was well enough pleased with the proposition; but when my mother said she could not go with me, I very unwillingly consented to the journey, for I was never so easy and so pleased as when I was under my mother's care.

But when the time came that Valeria and I must part, and I found how hard it was to bear the absence of a friend, I almost repented me I had ever loved her, and then I should never have known the misery of being from a person that is one's soul's delight. But she was less wretched than I was because she went with a husband that was infinitely fond of her. But why should I dwell on a subject that made me so melancholy, and not entertain you with my adventures, that perhaps may be more diverting to you?

One evening I went with Valeria and Silvanus to walk in the park, and in the dark walk we encountered Colonel Harnando. He saluted Silvanus and congratulated his happiness. He was obliged to present Valeria to him, and I being in the company, he also saluted me. This unexpected adventure had like to have produced but bad effects, for all on a sudden I was quite dispirited, and I had like to have fainted away, which Valeria perceiving, pulled me by the sleeve, and bid me go along with her. We left the two sparks a-talking, and Silvanus told me afterwards that Harnando asked my name and was very scrutinous in his inquiry of me, but he only gave him this answer, that I was a particular friend of Valeria's. I know not what excited him to this curiosity — whether it was through sympathy of our former amours, or out of a natural curiosity to know the name of a new face — but his inquiry very much perplexed me. We had not walked twice the length of that walk but hard by the bird cage we met Philander, and he, having forgot his resolution of traveling as he promised when he parted last from me, accosted me with his usual gayety and flutt'ring way. He engaged himself in a discourse with Valeria and myself and so walked along with us. I asked him if the park had not been the furthest extent of his travels, for I could not imagine that in so short a time since I saw him, that he had crossed the seas twice. He replied pleasantly that being banished from my presence, it had the same effect on him as if he had traveled all the world over; and in obedience to my severe commands, he had endeavoured to forget me, though with much difficulty and reluctance he had attempted it; but if I would please to give him leave to wait on me, I should find him the most obsequious of my servants. After this manner did he entertain us till we came out of the park.

But the next day Sir Formal, according to his method, came to wait on me, and was very importunate with my mother to lay her commands on me to marry him; but my mother's dislike to him was as great as mine, and she flatly refused his propositions and civilly desired him to withdraw from her house. But he would go on in his way, and would not balk his method for anyone's pleasure. Therefore did I resolve to go into the country to be rid of his importunity, and Valeria being gone, I may say the town all on a sudden became a desert. I prepared myself therefore for my journey and never spoke a word of my intentions to Sir Formal, but places were taken in the stagecoach for Iris and myself. I had no regret in leaving the town but upon the account of my mother, to whom in my absence I ever feared some accident or other might happen, she being very sickly. The grief was great on both sides to part, but with much ado we did, and went to our coach, where we were told that at Highgate we should take up two passengers.

What happened to me in my journey, my dear Indamora, I will acquaint you in my next, though I believe I have formerly told you the adventure; but since you desire a history of my life, I will not omit the least circumstance that is of moment; and I hope sometime or other, you will repay me with an account of your own life, which is a mixture of such variety of fortune, that it will oblige me to be acquainted with the particulars, which I can only know from yourself. And as I am a passionate lover of my Indamora, I may challenge this favour as due to the friendship I have for her. Who am most entirely her

Friend and servant,
Lindamira

THE END OF THE FIRST PART OF THE ADVENTURES OF LINDAMIRA

Letter VII

The parting from my mother, my dear Indamora, was a very great affliction to me, and I had scarce dried up my tears when I came to Highgate, where the coachman was to take in two passengers more. He stopped at the house according to order; and there came into the coach two gentlemen, one of 'em a very grave sort of a man and pretty well advanced in years, the other in the prime of his youth, of a graceful, winning behaviour. He was of a middle size, exactly well-shaped, his hair brown, a good complexion, sparkling eyes, and the whole composure of his face was lovely; there was an invincible charm in everything he said or did, and his extraordinary good breeding added much to his natural beauty.

I have, my Indamora, given you a full description of his person, but to complete his character I must not omit the excellencies of his mind, though at my first acquaintance, you may suppose, I did not make a full discovery of 'em. He was of an equal temper, had a passionate and tender soul; he was incapable of the least envy or slander, nor would he be guilty of a base action to purchase the greatest fortune imaginable. Though he was owner of many virtues, he did not affect to discover his perfections but to those he was very familiar with. In short, besides his mastership of the ancient and modern languages, he had a sound and solid judgment. I might ascribe

41

many virtues more to him, but I have said enough of Cleomidon to make you know him.

The first day's journey I exchanged but few words with him, for my eyes were so swollen with crying that I had not assurance enough to look him in the face, nor was it possible for me that night to have given a description of his person. The next day he entertained me with very diverting, ingenious sort of discourse and seemed to bear a share in the concern I expressed to leave my mother, telling me it was necessary sometimes to part from our friends to endear us the more when we meet; that absence helped to quicken and sharpen our affections, and till we come to know the want of a friend, we did not know how to value him. He was very entertaining and agreeable upon this occasion; and since I have obliged myself to discover my most secret sentiments to you, I thought him a person that merited my esteem. But having a strong fancy or rather an unquiet sort of an apprehension that Cleomidon was married, I durst not give way to admire those excellencies I discovered in him, for I had not forgot my unhappy affection for the Colonel.

The next night when we were just arrived at our inn we saw a coach with a gentleman and his wife enter the yard. Cleomidon, accidentally seeing of 'em, went up to 'em and saluted 'em. They proved to be his intimate friends, who were going to London; and there not being any likelihood of meeting a long time, Cleomidon invited 'em to sup with him, and bespoke a supper that showed the nobleness of his mind. He sent me word of his good fortune in meeting with his friends, and desired me to give 'em leave to sup with me. This request I could not handsomely refuse, and therefore went to wait on the lady in her chamber, who being left alone (for her husband was in another room with Cleomidon), I found an occasion to mention him; and this lady, being a person of a free and open temper, told me as much of him as she knew: that he was a barrister of Lincoln's Inn, that his father and mother died when he was young, that he had a free, unincumbered, though small estate, that his uncle (to whom he was going) had educated him as his own, and designed to leave him all his estate when he died if he pleased him in his marriage, and that he had sent for him this vacation, to see a young lady of a considerable fortune but of slender education.

All this she frankly told me without the least question on my side. As I was glad to hear he was not a married man, I could not forbear to be concerned at the news that he was going to see a fortune, knowing what invincible charms there is in money. This uneasiness I had in my mind was unaccountable, nor could I discover why I did interess myself so much in his affairs. But at supper I observed him more than I had done before, which confirmed me in the good opinion I had of him; for his freedom and easiness with his friends and his obliging way of entertaining 'em extremely affected me.

The next day, which was the last of our journey together, Cleomidon told me, sighing, that it was an unspeakable affliction to him to think that this was the last day he was like to be happy in my company, and that though he had but a small acquaintance with me, yet he had discovered something in my humour that to him was charming. It would be needless to repeat the compliments that fell from him upon this article, some of which were so extravagantly pursued, that I had reason to doubt if he spoke the sincerity of his heart, since he was so liberal of his incense to a stranger, and treated me all the while at the expense of the rest of my sex. So all this I looked upon as gallantry and the inclination most young people have. When we came to our inn at night, he drew me aside to a window that looked into the garden, and asked me if I had no mind to take a walk, for the air was calm and serene. I refused his offer, alleging I was tired with my long journey. He then said to me the most passionate and most obliging things in the world, assuring me he was charmed the first minute he beheld me, that he dated his captivity from that interview, that my tears had wrought a strange compassion in his heart, which insensibly gave way to esteem and admiration, that he was already become the most passionate, most sincere lover in the universe; and though he dreaded my anger for this presumptuous declaration, yet he was willing to undergo the most severest punishment I could inflict, if I would give him leave to hope one day he might be happy in my favour. I must confess my astonishment was very great to hear him speak this with so serious an air, for what he had said to me in the coach I ascribed to the gayety of his temper, but now was convinced he had some affection for me. I had too great an esteem to be offended at this *éclaircissement*. I evaded as much as I could the answering his compliments, thinking it necessary to observe those punctilios of our sex, which at the first discovery of a passion obliges us to keep our favour at a distance. I disengaged myself as soon as possible, and would not give him any farther opportunity of speaking to me in private that night.

At supper he said little to me but let his eyes speak for him. When news was brought my grandmother's coach was come, his countenance altered, and he seemed extremely troubled. I could not but take notice of the change I observed in his face, and I found some regret in my own soul to part from him. But when the next morning came, he found an opportunity of representing to me the greatness of his passion, and said so many kind and obliging things, that to doubt of his sincerity was to suppose him of a base mean spirit and that he only said these things for his amusement; but I had nobler thoughts of one that appeared so worthy of my esteem. When I was to go away, he offered his hand to lead me down the stairs and then told me he never was sensible of the power of love till now, but then began to feel the tyranny of it, and begged of me by all the kindest, softest words he could invent, to give him leave to wait on me at my grandmother's house, for 'twas a place he was no stranger to. I apprehended no little danger from his visits, knowing the temper of my grandmother, who was of a very reserved humour and did not affect much company, and according to the genius of most persons of that complexion, though she was very religious, yet very censorious, for which reason I used all the arguments I could to divert him from coming. I rendered him all the acknowledgments that was due to his merits, and let him understand I was not altogether insensible of his favours, but as I lay under those circumstances of being with a relation of that humour (for whom I had a great respect), I begged of him to think no more of me; but those words drew from his mouth a thousand protestations of his love, and that he would adore me eternally though I was so cruel to deny him that favour.

Then I began to think my heart in danger, and I was forced to borrow from my reason all the arguments it could furnish me with; and already I perceived an affection that pleaded on his behalf, which made me strive with myself, though not without some reluctancy, to represent to him how disagreeable his visits would be to me. But here, my Indamora, I played a downright hypocrite; I spoke not the thoughts of my heart, for I desired nothing more than his charming conversation. However, I durst not consent to what was so agreeable to my inclinations, and I dreaded a second engagement, which I thought I ought not to make without the approbation of my mother.

On these terms we parted, and I believe the affliction was as great on my side, though I endeavoured to conceal it with more care. I was received by my grandmother with great civility and kindness, as also by my Uncle and Aunt B—— who was there at that time. The next day they showed me all the house and gardens, and told me they reserved one place more to show me the next day, which they did, and because the knowledge of my adventures somewhat depends upon a description of this place, I will give it you in as concise a manner as I can. This house was situated on the rise of a hill. At a convenient distance ran a river, which in the summertime rendered the place very delightful. Not far from it was a wood encompassing some few acres of ground, and in the midst of it a path that led to a little rivulet, near half a mile long, and a row of high elms on both sides, so that in the midst of the day one might walk without the least inconveniency from the weather. At the head of this rivulet was a well that was paved about with broad stone, and benches round, fixed there for the ease of those that out of curiosity came there to drink of the water, which had a great reputation for its extraordinary sweetness. A few paces from this well, after some turnings and windings, you come into a little solitary valley, at the end of which stands a small cottage, which formerly had been a place of retirement for a gentleman that passed his days in solitude, but now it became the habitation of some few peasants.

I was extremely pleased with this rural scene, and I proposed to myself to spend some hours there in an evening, for I thought it looked so romantic and pretty, and equaled the best descriptions I had ever read on. I expressed my inclination to it by my unwillingness to leave it, which surprised my uncle and aunt, who told me they did not imagine that a London lady could be so diverted with looking on trees and in hearing the birds sing, but were extremely pleased at it in hopes I would make a considerable stay in the country.

I began from that time to reflect on the innocence of a country life, and preferred it before the empty noise and bustle of the town. I according to this resolution walked out every evening with only Iris with me, to pass some moments in this valley, where it was no small diversion to hear the awkward, ill-contrived compliments that the clowns made on the little beauty of their mistresses, and their piping, squeaking, and dancing before 'em, and now and then out of abundance of love I should see those two-handed clodpates carry home their milk pails for 'em. Thus I diverted myself for a month, in which time I had heard no news of Cleomidon, so that I concluded he was either false, or had repented him of his weakness, or that the great fortune of his uncle's recommendation had produced the usual effects in his heart as it does in the rest of mankind and made him sacrifice all former vows and protestations. Though in strict justice I ought not to have expected it from him, having laid injunctions on him not to visit me, yet sometimes I wished he had not shown so implicit an obedience, and that he would have contrived some way to let me know I was not indifferent to him, which shortly after he did in a very odd and surprising manner. But I must digress a little before I can acquaint you with this adventure, that I may make you the better understand the capriciousness of my fortune. But as this letter, my Indamora, is already too long, I shall not here engage myself in the description of some people that I must give you till I have an opportunity to finish it. Adieu, my dearest Indamora.

I am yours, Lindamira

Letter VIII

MY DEAREST INDAMORA,

I have only two people whose characters I am to acquaint you with that lived in the house with my grandmother. One of 'em was her chaplain, a jolly young Levite, very amorous, and susceptible of love, his conversation not impertinent, and they tell me he passed amongst his brother Spintexts for a man of very good parts, and made no small figure at a country visitation. The other was a grave gentlewoman, my grandmother's everlasting confidante, and though she had passed the glory of her youth, yet she thought herself handsome enough to attract a lover. Her complexion was indifferent good, her skin smooth, her eyes brisk and lively, which showed her to be of a quick apprehension; her shape, though not exact, yet agreeable enough. Her humour had been very jocose and pleasant, but love had altered her before I knew her, and she put on an affected seriousness, and was naturally jealous of all her friends, and did entertain very extravagant notions of 'em that were inconsistent with reason.

This person, I know not for what design, made great professions of friendship to me, which I believe proceeded from noble charity, for I was young and inexperienced and did not apprehend the plots and stratagems that are laid underground to deceive the innocent, and therefore offered me her advice, both in the management of myself and in my affairs. I re-

ceived these marks of her esteem with all due acknowledgments and suffered myself to be guided by her advice, which
she was very free of, and would often repeat to me the sin of
giving way to passion, adding that she herself had been very
subject to it before she had read Seneca, and that she owed all
her moderation to that worthy Stoic, that now she could forgive offences with ease and despised the arts of envious
tongues and could bear detraction and calumny without concern. These virtues I highly applauded in her, and thought
her a woman the most worthy of my envy of any living, that
had gained so great a conquest over her passions, and told her
I wished I were capable of receiving those good instructions
she had given me. This pleased her so well that she lent me
the author of all her moderation, and supposing I was not ex-
empt from passions no more than the rest of our frail sex, she
told me she hoped I would receive great advantage from it,
and that she would have me read no other book till I had finished that.

About five days after, she came to visit me in my chamber
to learn what progress I had made and what effects it had
wrought upon my mind (as if a change of sentiment could
happen to one in an instant). But, my Indamora, admire at
my ill fate! For she found me reading of a romance, which
I was very intent upon, and being deeply engaged in the unfortunate adventures of a disconsolate lover, I minded her not
when she came in but continued my reading, and she, perceiving what my study was, assumed a supercilious look and
a contracted brow. "So, Lindamira," said she, "how much you
value my advice, that prefers the reading of an idle romance
before the precepts of the wise and learned Seneca! Take my
word," continued she, raising the tone of her voice; "nothing
so much corrupts the minds of young people as the reading of
these foolish books that treat of fulsome love and fills their
heads full of chimeras." I could not help laughing at my
friend for the wrong notions she had taken of the books that

so pleasantly had spun out my time, and I very ignorantly began to defend the wit of the ingenious author. But this sage lady, whose wisdom was much greater than my small experience, told me I should reap more advantage in one day in reading Seneca, Livy, Plutarch, or Tacitus than I could my whole life in such fabulous stories. But then being persuaded into an opinion of her high virtues and good humour, I did venture to entreat her to hear out the sequel of my story (for there was nothing that could offend her chaste ears) and did believe, notwithstanding her aversion to love, she had good nature enough to deplore the misfortunes of an unhappy lover that was made so by the rigour of his cruel mistress, and that the despairs she had put him into made me to compassionate his infelicities, and that I had not power to leave off till I saw the result of his destiny, whom I feared would be banished her sight forever. But instead of interesting her in these adventures, she very sharply reproved me, representing the ill consequences of employing my time so ill, and made such invectives against love and so protested against it that I thought her a mere Stoic indeed. But our disputes lasted so long that it was time to go walk, that I asked her if she would please to breathe the fresh air after our hot dispute. But she was so much out of humour for the contempt I showed of her advice that she refused to go with me. Her denial pleased me very well, for I took my book with me and finished what I designed as I walked in the shady grove. But from this time I altered my opinion of her; I neither believed her so great a saint nor a philosopher as she pretended, and my conjectures were not ill-grounded as it appeared a few days after.

But I will leave her awhile to fret whilst I relate my adventure with Mr. Spintext, the chaplain, who, unknown to me, was become my humble admirer. This Levite had often entertained me with his poetry, and Sylvia, Phillis, and Cloris were oftentimes repeated, that I supposed him a general lover of the sex. He would beg my opinion of his poems, and as I was no judge of the excellencies of his performances, I commended those verses the least elevated, and found the most fault where his flights were the most surprising. But these errors in my judgment he easily excused, as mountain faults in lovers' eyes seems but molehill, but still I did not suspect I was the theme of these compositions, till one morning that I was sitting in the summerhouse in the garden for the conveniency of my painting (there being a north light). I had only Iris with me and had not been there an hour but Mr. Spintext entered, under pretence of viewing my drawings (for I was then but a learner); but this obliging Levite commended what merited not his applauses, and admired as ignorantly my paintings as I his poetry.

From one discourse to another he fell upon that of love, and after he had fetched two or three deep sighs, which was the prologue to what he had to say, he told me I was infinitely esteemed by all that knew me, but in that numerous train of admirers none had a greater veneration for me than himself, and was very ambitious to be admitted into the catalogue of my humble servants, adding, with a sigh, that I was the sole object of his thoughts and the only theme of his poetry. I heard out his harangue without interrupting him, and expressed my resentments for his boldness in terms that sufficiently let him see how sensibly I was affronted that my grandmother's chaplain should dare to talk to me of love; saying that I thought myself in a sphere too high to be entertained by him with such discourse, that it became him much better to mind his flock and to give 'em spoon meat in due season, and that the greatest solecism a divine could be guilty of was to make love, and that people of his cloth should never condescend so low as to encourage a foolish passion, but entertain themselves with their fathers and councils.

I rallied him in this manner and made him sensible of his folly, for a guilty dumbness seized him. He said not one word to excuse or justify himself for what he had done. Seeing him so much out of countenance, I was almost sorry I said so much, but I was convinced in my own thoughts it was the best way to repress his boldness in the beginning. However, believing he might apprehend something from my displeasure and that I might acquaint my grandmother with what had passed, I satisfied him I had no design to do him a prejudice, provided he observed a due decorum in his actions for the future.

Now, my Indamora, do but observe what malignant planets reigned over me, for I had no sooner given over my reprimand to Mr. Spintext and had hardly composed my countenance but the disciple of Seneca entered, who you must know was secretly in love with this young Levite; and she, being older than he, was troubled with that pernicious disease called jealousy, and for some time had suspected he had an inclination for me, for she was eagle-eyed and had a quicker apprehension than myself. She observed him when he went into the garden, and he staying longer than in her wisdom she thought he ought, she put wings to her feet and came flying after, and was resolved to be an ocular witness of his deportment to me. When she first came in, I observed a disturbance in her eyes but could not conjecture the cause of it. I told her I was sorry she did not come sooner, for I had just finished what I designed to do, and that her company would have made the time pass more agreeably away.

But she answered my civility in a most surprising manner, and in an angry tone told me I had such good company with me, that if I had spoke the truth of my heart her absence would have been most pleasing to me, and that I knew, as young as I was, how to dissemble my thoughts. "What is your meaning, madam?" said I. "For I am as little guilty of dissimulation as anyone, and this is a great piece of injustice to accuse me wrongfully." "You are so insensible," replied she, "and pretend so much ignorance that 'twill be a difficult matter, I warrant you, to convince your ladyship that you are beloved by Mr. Spintext." "What if I be?" said I, hastily. "I hope, madam, it will give no chagrin if he could be guilty of so great a folly?" This answer did more inflame her anger, so that she forgot all her pretended patience and discretion, and, wholly abandoning herself to her fury, she multiplied her words so fast that she would repeat the same thing over several times. She told me I was young, foolish, and conceited of myself, and took a pleasure in hearing myself flattered and having amorous songs made of me, and that I encouraged Mr. Spintext in his pretensions of love to me. By this I perceived she had not heard our discourse, and it was only the effects of her jealousy that made her to accuse me, and therefore I would not acknowledge the truth, but in a bantering way demanded of her if I should not return her Seneca's *Morals,* for I feared through the defect of her memory she had forgot how great a sin it was to give way to passion, and that it was also injurious to beauty, and that the fault was greater in her, who had made such solemn professions of moderation and all that, than in others who were so sincere as to own the frailties of their nature.

She was so transported by her anger that it choked her words, and she stamped and stared about the room, she hurried up and down like a frantic Bacchanal. At last she was forced to have recourse to her tears, which fell in such abundance from her eyes that she represented old Hecuba in the play. And on a sudden the sky was calm and serene, and she dried up her tears with her dirty handkerchief, and giving a sudden turn towards Mr. Spintext, she darted fiery looks at him and thundered in his ears such peals of her indignation that she amazed him in such sort, that I never see one look so astonished as he did; for till that time he was ignorant of the violent affection she had for him. But she so ill expressed her passion that she served for an antidote against it. But during this long conversation she acted the part so well of an indefatigable talker and a most unequalled scold that from that time I ever called her Xantippe, who was wife to Socrates of patient memory.

That evening I related to Olympia (my grandmother's

woman) this surprising adventure, telling her how much I was mistaken in the humour of Xantippe, whom till then I believed to be a woman of great discretion and prudence, but in this emergency she behaved herself like one that had neither sense nor reason. Olympia replied that I was not the only person that had been mistaken in her, for the character she had given of herself had deceived many, and she was of a humour not to bear a contradiction but always acted a superior's part to those she honoured with her favour. But from that time I esteemed her less than anyone and looked upon her as a dangerous acquaintance, for in her passion she was guilty of detraction to the last degree, that I was ever after only civil to her, with thanks returned her book again. You may judge, my Indamora, she was not a person in whom I durst confide, and after that I entertained myself more with Olympia, who was wellborn and virtuously educated and had a genius less morose and more conformable to my own humour.

Thus have I given you a faithful account of what passed till that time without concealing my most secret thoughts, which is the greatest proof I can give of my sincere affection to my Indamora, to whom I am

A faithful, humble servant,
Lindamira

Letter IX

It will be time now, my Indamora, to acquaint you after what manner I was surprised with the sight of Cleomidon, who during my stay at Palarmo had not heard any news of him. One Sunday being at church, I observed an awkward sort of a country clown who unalterably kept his eyes fixed on me. His dress was that of the meanest peasants, and nothing drew my eyes towards him but his continual staring at me. When sermon was done, I met him in the church porch, who made me several reverend scrapes with his hat to the ground. I could not help smiling at his officious care to make me look at him, which I did without the least suspicion whom he was. Before I was got into the coach, he whispered to Iris (in giving her two letters): "For heaven's sake, dear Iris," said he, "give this to Lindamira." Her surprise was so great that she let the letters fall, but he gave 'em her again without the least observation by Xantippe, who was just by her. As soon as we came home and that I was in my chamber, she presented them to me, telling me in what manner she received 'em. My astonishment was greater than can be imagined. I knew not what to do in this emergency nor what to think of this adventure, but at last I took courage to open the letter and found these words from the faithful Cleomidon.

CLEOMIDON TO LINDAMIRA

Never did soul feel such anguish as mine did that ill-boding

morning that robbed me of your sight. All things seemed to
join to wrack me, already too much oppressed with grief, so
that I left untold a thousand fond things my soul was full of.
Madam, be just to my passion and reward it with a return
suitable to my sincerity of it. If my prayers or wishes be the
least prevailing, let me receive an answer, and deny not the
happiness of an hour's conversation to him that would sacrifice his life in your service.

Adieu

I read this letter over a hundred times, revolving in my
thoughts what I should do, and 'twas a long time before I
could come to any resolution; but the result was that I would
return him an answer by Iris, to whom he wrote also to inform her where to inquire for him. It is impossible for you to
conceive, unless you had seen as I did, that a man that was
genteel, of a noble presence, and who had so particular an
obligingness with him, could so alter himself by his dress. For
'twas Cleomidon that was in this disguise, which he put on to
facilitate his design, being resolved to see me, and durst not
appear in his own shape for fear of giving some suspicion. I
was in some inquietudes about him, for I had more than a
common esteem for him, but I durst not indulge my inclination, because that at Palarmo a visitor of that sex would have
been a very great crime; therefore I gave him no encouragement to make a second attempt to see me, and only wrote him
these few words.

LINDAMIRA TO CLEOMIDON

Is it possible that absence has not proved an effectual cure
for your passion, since I have already told you I will not bestow my heart without the approbation of her that has it entirely at her devotion? I have commanded Iris to acquaint you
with my reasons why I cannot gratify your request, which
must be to the hazard of my honour and reputation. If you

have that esteem for me which you profess, you cannot take unkindly so reasonable a denial.

Farewell

When Iris demanded for Cleomidon by the name he mentioned and he came to her, she could not believe it was he, for not only his countenance was altered but the tone of his voice, which he had so well counterfeited that 'twas impossible to know him. But he soon delivered her out of the uncertainties he was in by speaking to her in his own natural voice (which was sweet, yet not effeminate). "Dear Iris," said he, "what news do you bring from Lindamira? Can she pardon me this device I have made use on to see her? For seriously," continued he, "I have not had one hour's repose since I saw her, and all the *divertissements* and caresses of my friends and relations have not been able to drive her idea from my mind." Iris then gave him my letter, for which favour he expressed much acknowledgment; but when he had read it over and saw I had denied his request, he seemed like a man distracted. "Is there no means, Iris," said he, "that I may possibly speak to Lindamira and she run no hazard of her reputation, which is dear to me next to her life?" Iris represented to him that if my grandmother should ever know it, I should lose her favour forever. But he expostulated with her so long and used so many enforcing arguments to add her endeavour to bring him to a sight of me, that the poor Iris at last being overcome by his great impressment, that she promised she would use her interest to persuade me to meet him in the valley at the end of the wood, but she so much apprehended the consequence of its being known that she already dreaded the encounter.

At her return she related all that had passed, adding many things in favour of him, and pleaded so well in his behalf and so effectually laid before me his impatience of seeing me that I yielded to her request, and in the evening, according to our wonted custom, we went to take our walk. But when I came into the valley and bethought myself that I came to meet a gentleman with whom I had but a small acquaintance, I reproached myself for my weakness, that I should suffer the persuasions of Iris to work any effect upon my mind, and I was just upon making a retreat and resolved to turn back, when at the same instant I perceived Cleomidon come from behind a great oak tree that had sheltered him from my sight. He perceiving my intentions advanced towards me with much precipitation, saying, "Madam, do you shun me? What cruel destiny is mine? Is this all I am to hope? For heaven's sake hear me speak, my Lindamira!" I made a stop at these words, nor had I power to go, and by my silence he might judge his sight was not unpleasing to me. Though I ought to have condemned him for this boldness, yet when I looked on him I discovered so much love and passion in his eyes I had not the heart to make him any reproaches. He said to me the most passionate things imaginable and represented his own misfortunes, after so feeling, so sensible a manner, of being so long deprived of the sight of me, that I thought there was no room left for doubt but that his heart and his lips agreed, for such was the powerful rhetoric of love that I believed Cleomidon could not be guilty of a falsehood. To remove my wonder for the extraordinary kindness he expressed, which I seemed to doubt of, he told me it was not strange to see that love at its first birth should sometimes arrive at all its perfection, which time and a greater knowledge do generally give it. "For," pursued he, "I love you to that degree that 'twas impossible my passion should admit of an increase."

Cleomidon afterwards related to me all that the lady at the inn had acquainted me with, but slightly ran over the design his uncle had to marry him to Cleodora. I was, I confess, very scrutinous in my inquiry into what perfections this lady had and what recommendable qualities she had to subdue a heart, and as her fortune was very considerable, I did fear it might shock his constancy, but to remove those doubts he would often say that since he had seen Lindamira, he could not be pleased with any other, and added so many obliging expressions in favour of me that I had no suspicion but that he spoke his real thoughts.

Our conversation lasted above two hours, and I must own to you without shame and confusion that those amiable qualities I discovered in him wrought a greater effect on my heart than they ought; that being conscious to myself I ought not to have engaged my affections without my mother's knowledge, I was extremely troubled to find that my heart was no longer at her disposal. But the humour of Cleomidon was the most gallant, the most agreeable, and most diverting of any man in the world. He has naturally an eloquence so easy and fluent that few persons can explain their conceptions after a more entertaining manner than himself. I could not, after I had thoroughly considered them, but acknowledge I was not insensible of his affection. He made me vows of his eternal fidelity, that nothing should be able to shock his constancy. I answered him in the most obliging terms I could, and gave him leave to hope that if my mother should approve of his affection, he should not find me ungrateful; and I begged of him to be content with that esteem I had for him, and had promised to answer his letters, and though he lived but twenty miles from Palarmo, yet our letters were to pass by London for fear of giving a suspicion. After we had settled this correspondence, I told him it was time for me to return home, it being suppertime, and I saw by my watch I had already outstayed my time; but the word "depart" extremely troubled him, and he durst not in prudence press me to stay. I left him, I must acknowledge, with much reluctancy, and him no less concerned for this separation.

But when I came home, I found my grandmother at supper, from whom I received a severe chastisement, for in my absence Xantippe had aggravated my being out so late as a very criminal matter, which possessed my grandmother with some unusual disquiets, and had sent a servant in quest of me. I hearkened to all that was said with much patience and was glad I had escaped without being discovered, that I was very silent and wholly abandoned my thoughts to Cleomidon. After supper I retired into my chamber, where I had the liberty to recollect in my thoughts this evening's adventure, and upon examination of my heart I found all the signs of a tender and sincere affection, and wished to reign absolute in his without the cruel apprehensions of a rival rich and fair as was Cleodora.

This was the condition of my soul when I was so happy to see my dear Indamora at that delicious place Lauretta, where a few days after this adventure happened to me. I waited on my grandmother to see Lucretia, and from that time I may date my happiness in your friendship, in whose agreeable conversation I passed away three weeks; and though at the first interview I had a great esteem for you, yet I did not acquaint you with the affection I had for Cleomidon, lest you should disapprove of my conduct. But you may perhaps remember something of the relation I have given of Philander and Sir Formal, but you telling me you had forgot the particulars of their amours, I thought it not unnecessary to the completing of my adventures to bring them in their proper places.

Your goodness has made you commend what merited not your praises, and your indulgence to my ill performance encourages me still to go on, that you may command from my pen whatever is worthy of your knowledge; but I owe much to your good humour, and am without compliment, with all the sincerity as may be,

My dearest Indamora,
Your true and faithful Lindamira

Letter X

Whilst I was at Lauretta, my dear Indamora, I wrote to Cleomidon and gave him an account how happy I was in a new friend I had gained since I came to that place. I will not tell you what I said of you, because your modesty will not bear the just praises of your friends; but in answer to that letter he said he was charmed with the character of her I mentioned, but looked upon her as a dangerous friend, because she had robbed him of part of my soul. Though I received this answer whilst I was at Lauretta, I said not one syllable of it to you. Being of a humour not to be very free till I am intimately acquainted, I left untold several things that I wished since I had informed you of. And for the time I have been known to you, you have gained a greater interest in my heart than anyone except my dear Valeria, for whom I had, and have still, a great value and esteem; but she being married and much taken up with her domestic affairs, I seldom heard from her whilst I was at Palarmo, nor durst I acquaint her with anything concerning Cleomidon, fearing lest my letters might come to the view of Silvanus. When I went from Lauretta, you best can tell with what unwillingness I parted from so agreeable a society and what was my grief to leave so charming a friend; for at my return to Palarmo I was to converse with a jealous, forward, and impertinent woman (without any further pursuit of her character you may guess her to be Xantippe). For ever since she treated me so liberally with her billingsgate in the summerhouse, she began to hate me, and clandestinely did me all the ill offices she could to my grandmother, though to my face she was civil, but jealous of my power, which she thought greater than her own. But her humour made me not uneasy, for my thoughts were wholly taken up upon a subject more worthy of my love and friendship, and I often received news from Cleomidon, who still continued his affection and failed not to give me all the assurances of an unalterable love, that I read over his letters with delight and answered 'em with pleasure, so that the time passed away as agreeably as 'twas possible in the absence of the person loved.

But now I must say something of Mr. Spintext, who was a man that had many good qualities, I mean that fell under my notice and observation. His only fault was owning his love for me, for which it seemed he was extremely troubled, and told Iris of it, wishing he could have an opportunity to beg my pardon and acknowledge his fault. He owned indeed that he could not repent that he loved me but that he had displeased me in acquainting me with it; but for the future he would be as silent as the night if he could but once but ease his mind of the pain and anguish he did labour under. But though Iris told me this, I was unwilling to gratify his request upon the account of Xantippe's jealous humour, whom I knew was very watchful both of him and me, and as I had long since forgot his crime, I thought it not necessary to let him speak to me.

About a month after my return to Palarmo, I received the surprising news that Cleomidon lay concealed in the little cottage that is in the valley. He sent me a billet wherein he conjured me not to refuse him the sight of me once more, deploring his unhappiness that he had not the freedom of waiting on me at my grandmother's house that he might publicly own the passion he had for me, and was grieved that he was put to the necessity of desiring me to meet him, when it was his part to have come all the way. But these niceties are easily sacrificed to love, and I found arguments enough to palliate his fault; and wishing to see him (though at the hazard of my grandmother's displeasure), I sent him word I would meet him at the well, which place being more public I thought less dangerous in case anyone should perceive me talking to him. With Iris I went, and when I came to the place of assignation, I saw Cleomidon lie fast asleep upon one of the benches of the well. He since told me he had stayed so long waiting for me that his spirits were tired with expectation, that he laid him down in hopes to sleep, to delude the tedious hours. But I had then the satisfaction of looking on him with more attention than ever I had done yet, and the more I viewed him, the more I was confirmed in the good opinion I had of him; but fearing he might awake and find me in this contemplating posture, I walked away and bid Iris awake him, for I had no time to lose. She no sooner obeyed me, but he starting up, and seeing only her by him, he expressed in his eyes all the marks of despair. But Iris took compassion on him and told him I was hard by, which restored him to his former tranquillity of mind, and seeing me coming towards him, he ran to me and with open arms received me, saying the most kindest, tenderest words that his passion could furnish him with. I faintly reproached him for his returning again, alleging what hazard I ran for his sake; but he wanted not expressions to excuse himself, for love made him so eloquent and acknowledging, that I could not be angry at him. 'Tis endless to repeat what vows of fidelity he made me that nothing should shock his constancy; I on my side gave him all the innocent marks of an affection that I thought might be justifiable to the world. He told me he designed to be in London in three weeks and did hope he might persuade me to hasten my return thither; but then I had not thoughts of going so soon as it afterwards fell out.

After this manner we passed our time, and the hours glided pleasantly away, when at a distance I discovered Mr. Spintext, who directed his steps that way. I interrupted Cleomidon, telling him whom I saw and that I feared my grandmother had sent him after me, it being near suppertime. But this adventure did so sour his joys and justled all those thoughts out of his mind that he designed to have acquainted me with, which too late I knew afterwards; but the approach of this unwelcome divine made us resolve to separate, and I assured Cleomidon I would follow him into the valley as soon as I had learned what his errand was, but I then little apprehended he came upon his own. At his approach to me I read in his eyes some concern and was afraid to know the truth, being only apprehensive upon Cleomidon's account. But he soon delivered me out of that perplexity and drove me into another, for this was the fatal time, my Indamora, that he took to make his recantation and to beg my pardon for his temerity, assuring me he was so sensible of the offence he had given me in suffering his thoughts to roam beyond a sphere too great for him; but as his judgment was not in fault, he hoped I would have some indulgence for his crime. He expressed himself in a very pathetical strain and made very ingenuous acknowledgments of his faults, that had my resentments lasted till that time, I must have pardoned him, and did assure him I would, provided he observed that decorum that became him. As I ended these words I rose up with an intention to be gone, not giving him leave to prolong the discourse, when at a distance I discovered a creature make towards me, who rather flew than went on feet, but so far off I could not well distinguish what it was, that I concluded it was some hobgoblin or some winged monster of the night, for there appeared nothing of human in the shape or form of it. I stopped awhile to behold what this Proteus might be, for it appeared in several shapes, but as it nearer did approach my eye I saw it was a woman. But to complete my ill fortune it was the terrible Xantippe, whom rage and jealousy had led thither, and with all the fury of a woman in despair came to reproach Mr. Spintext with his ingratitude to her and me with my intrigues with him. But as I thought it not consistent with prudence to retreat, believing that she knew me, I took a resolution to stand the brunt of her anger, though Mr. Spintext would have persuaded me to have shunned the storms that threatened me.

No sooner did this furioso approach me, though quite out of breath, but she darted fire from her eyes, which prepared me to hear her thunder; and as her voice was shrill and loud enough upon occasion, it was so now, more than ordinary; for being possessed with an unaccountable jealousy, she gave a loose to all her thoughts and quite forgot her boasted moderation. Such streams of words flowed from her tongue, that 'twas amazing where she found expressions so suitable to her passion; but the rage of Juno was not greater when Paris give the apple from her than was Xantippe to see her dearly beloved divine so near to me. And after she had recovered breath, she told me she thought herself bound in gratitude to my grandmother to take some care of me, for she perceived my walks was not designed so much for my health as to give Mr. Spintext an opportunity to court me. At last said I, "Madam, you are in as pleasant a humour today as when I saw you last in the summerhouse. I wish you were always thus diverting, and I would contribute what lay in my power to give you subject for your mirth." But surely never woman was so enraged and so diverted of all reason; for she acted the part of a frantic creature, and began to roll her eyes about and rose up hastily and came towards me, I suppose, with a design to play at pullquoif with me. But her career was stopped by Mr. Spintext interposing between, who then thought it high time to give her a gentle correction for her immoderate anger, which he did in a very mild way, and at last did reduce her to some reason, for she made him no reply but watered the mossy bank whereon she sat with her precious tears.

As soon as I thought the moisture of her eyes was exhaled, and that to her passion she had given vent enough, "Come, let's be gone, madam," said I, "for what will my grandmother say that we are out so late? And what excuse can you make?" But this sage lady only answered me with an ominous look, and, leading the way, she followed me. I failed not to entertain Mr. Spintext as I went along, which I suppose she never could forgive. But all this while the poor Cleomidon suffered disquiets that cannot be expressed; I therefore whispered to Iris to go to him and give him an account of this unlucky accident, adding that the next day I would surely write to him.

When I came home I found my grandmother much out of humour that I was out so late, and to excuse and palliate my fault I said that Xantippe was with me; but she, like an indiscreet and malicious creature, retorted that by accident she met with me and Mr. Spintext, and thinking it not convenient for me to be alone with him, she stayed out the longer to keep me company, and that I had sent Iris to go home another way.

I was never more perplexed than at that time, not knowing what defence to make, for the truth I durst not own, and my countenance betrayed some guilt, which my grandmother observed, and was confirmed in a belief that I had made an appointment with Mr. Spintext, and therefore in a very angry tone forbade me ever walking there again unless Xantippe would do me the favour to bear me company. I replied she should be obeyed, that I never more would frequent a place that had caused her so much displeasure.

Soon after I retired, and Iris not being returned, I had a thousand fears she should be discovered; but I was soon after released from all my cares, for her sight filled my heart with a joy unspeakable. She recounted to me the vexation this disappointment had caused in the soul of Cleomidon, who depended much upon the promise I had made him of writing to him the next morning, which I failed not to do, with the assurance of my eternal fidelity to him.

Iris, who carried this letter, found Cleomidon a-walking in the valley in expectation of her. As soon as he had read over my letter (which seemed to please him), he sat him down under an oak tree, and returned me an answer that gave me all the reason in the world to believe that his fidelity was unshaken, and nothing could be more tender and kind than what he wrote to me. He pressed me much to hasten my journey to London, and that I would ever preserve him entirely in my heart.

After this adventure I should not have taken any pleasure in those shady walks though I had not been forbidden by my grandmother, and should have banished myself, for since this accident Palarmo seemed very dull to me. But as reading and my painting was my greatest diversions, I conversed very little with anyone, and with Xantippe the least, for this philosophical lady had given me a very bad opinion of all pretenders to philosophy, that I made those books the least of my study and took an opinion they were the least useful of any I could read. But it was my ignorance and her immoderation that made me despise the most profitable authors. But I will not longer entertain you with my sentiments upon that matter, but will finish this, with the assurance of my ever being,

My dear Indamora's
Most affectionate and faithful Lindamira

Letter XI

Knowing that Cleomidon designed for London in a short time, I resolved, my dear Indamora, to write to my mother to send for me away, which accordingly I did, and in ten days received an answer that I should prepare myself for my journey but was first to expect another letter; and being deprived of my usual diversion, I began to study mischief.

And as I was but too sensible that Xantippe had lessened me in the esteem of my grandmother (who through her means had entertained some unjust suspicions on me), I resolved to quit scores with her and requite all her civility at once. For as I've told you, Xantippe had a most violent affection for Mr. Spintext, and he no esteem for her; so I represented to myself no small satisfaction to see this furious lady deprived of all her hopes (though they were ill-grounded). And therefore I spoke to a gentleman who had some influence on the mind of this young Levite to buzz in his head that Olympia would make him a very good wife, who was pretty, very discreet, and much esteemed on by my grandmother, that 'twas probable for her sake he might get preferment, being she had a good living at her disposal. This I said to his friend, who had sense enough to know how to amplify matters and show 'em in the most advantageous situation; and he being young and susceptible of love, I fancied my plot might take. On the other hand I knew that Olympia had no disesteem for Mr. Spintext and therefore might be persuaded to admit him as a lover.

I no sooner mentioned this, but it was proposed to this worthy Levite, who at the first slighted his friend's advice, but being pressed to consider his own advantage, he at last resolved to try his fortune in hopes to succeed better than in his last amour. And at the same time I prevailed with Olympia to receive his addresses favourably; and I having some power with her, Mr. Spintext met with no great opposition in his courtship, for they having known each other a good while, there was no need of frivolous compliments. The first opportunity I confirmed him in the good choice he had made, and that I thought Olympia a person very worthy and deserving, and my friendship to her would make me the more assiduous in promoting his interest to my grandmother, which I hoped to do effectually when once they were married, which I wished might be before I went to London.

A few days after, this marriage was consummated, and with all the secrecy imaginable, without giving the least suspicion of any such design, and though Xantippe was like Argus with his hundred eyes and rolled 'em up and down in every place, yet was she blind to this affair, which gave no little joy to our bride and bridegroom, to whom was observed all the formalities at a wedding. For there was bride-cake, sack-posset, and flinging of the stocking, and none there but the bridegroom's friend, myself, Iris, and one maid.

You may perhaps wonder how this could be done without the knowledge of the eagle-eyed Xantippe, and yet we were all too cunning for her. But as 'twas necessary my grandmother should be acquainted with this marriage, I took my opportunity in the absence of Xantippe to let her know of it and withal to beg both their pardons, that they did not know of their design. Though this news was surprising to my grandmother, and perhaps at another time would have resented it, yet I could discover a secret joy in her countenance that her chaplain had disposed of himself, for Xantippe had lain a train of designs to destroy me in my grandmother's good opinion.

She then asked me where they were that she might wish 'em joy. I went immediately to 'em to let 'em know the favour that was designed 'em and to prepare 'em for this interview.

When they made their appearance, they both begged my grandmother's pardon that they had not asked her approbation and consent; but she very obligingly saluted the bride and, turning to the bridegroom, wished 'em both much happiness together. In this interim, Xantippe entered at another door and stood like one amazed, revolving in her mind what was the meaning of this salutation, for being ignorant of the marriage she did not presently apprehend it. But when she did, she was like one in Bethlehem, for she threw her eyes about, grinned with her teeth, stamped with her feet, and in short showed all the marks of a despairing creature; but she was under some restrictions, being in my grandmother's presence, or I believe she would have pulled their eyes out. This was so amazing to my grandmother, who was a stranger to her passions, that of a long time she could not speak but at last turning towards her, "Do you know, Lindamira," said she, "the reason that Xantippe looks so disturbed?" "Alas! Madam," said I, "her disorder proceeds from love, despair, and jealousy; for, madam, she was in love with Mr. Spintext and would have been glad to have been in Olympia's place." I spoke this I confess in a malicious tone and did ridicule her grief so much that, having lost all patience, she set no bounds to her anger, and without making any reply (for her precious tears had stopped her speech), she slipped off her shoe and flung it designedly at my head, but missing her aim, it lighted on the chimney piece amongst the china, which tumbled down great part that was there, which made so great a noise and a disturbance, that what with her sobs and dismal sighs this was a scene of disorder and distraction.

But what were my grandmother's thoughts in this emergency I can't well tell. But she could not but see she was deceived in her opinion of Seneca's disciple. But after some time

Xantippe began to recollect what she had done and, being ashamed of her ridiculous behaviour, withdrew out of the room with much precipitation, and in her haste tumbled down a chair or two, and having but one shoe on, she hobbled away in a very ungraceful manner and went into her closet, locked her door, where 'tis supposed after she had vented her sorrow, she considered that the world was full of disappointments, and there was no true happiness to be found. For four days she continued in this contemplating humour and conversed with nothing but Seneca; and during this happy truce I failed not of my design of prevailing with my grandmother to bestow that living she had in her gift on Mr. Spintext. My request was granted without much difficulty, and I saw a prospect of this couple's living happily together.

But when Xantippe made her appearance again (not being without the sense of shame), she looked very much out of countenance and dejected, that I almost repented me of what I had done. But my mirth cost me dear, for I then received a letter from a friend of my mother's that acquainted me of her being taken very ill, and that I must come away with all the speed imaginable. This news struck me with such a sadness and so sensible a grief that I hardly knew what I said or did, for I was ever very apprehensive how great my loss would be in the death of my mother. This news caused a general disturbance in the family, and my absence a grief to all but Xantippe. I left Palarmo without regret, for having lost the greatest part of my pleasure, since I did not frequent the grove, I had no other grief than that of leaving a very kind relation, but was going to one more dearer to me.

From that fatal journey I may date all my unhappiness, for then began the greatest change in my affairs. And what afterwards befell me when I came to London, I shall reserve for a more convenient opportunity, and though some years are passed since, yet I cannot think on that great misfortune without some sense of trouble. I find myself already too much affected with the thoughts of it, so will reserve that adventure for a more proper opportunity; and must also beg my dear Indamora's pardon for all faults, and being assured of your goodness I shall only assure you,

I am,

Your affectionate friend
and servant, Lindamira

THE END OF THE SECOND PART OF THE ADVENTURES OF LINDAMIRA

Letter XII

Never was soul possessed with such just apprehensions as I was for the sickness of my mother; for when I came to London, my dearest Indamora, I received the unwelcome news of her being in a dangerous condition. Her joy of seeing me, she said, gave her new life; but 'twas but a vapour, for she soon returned to her fainting fits again, of which she had many in a day. But I received from her all the marks of a tender affection; and during her intervals she failed not of giving me those necessary instructions for the conduct of myself, adding also that if I married, she wished I might make choice of one who had principles of honour and generosity and would scorn a base action, but left me to my own liberty. I found that her sentiments were still the same as mine, and did believe the humour of Cleomidon would answer the character she gave of one that might make me happy; but I had not courage to acquaint her with his affection to me, but deferred it till such time that I might, without inconveniency to herself, give an account of the whole affair.

In the meantime, I heard every day from Cleomidon but would not admit of a visit from him in the condition my mother was; for I was never a minute from her bedside. But as lovers are sometimes more impatient than others, he could not absent himself any longer from me. But that day he came to see me, it fell out unhappily for us both; for scarce had he been with me a quarter of an hour but I was called away in all haste. Being alarmed that my mother was a-dying, I almost lost my senses at this summons, but calling up all my courage, I ran to her to assist her the best I could. She was then but in a fit and recovered out of that in a short time after; but they returned upon her so fast, as all that night she hardly knew anyone, but the next day was much better and spoke to me of several things. Finding that she was not long for this world, "My dear child," said she, "take that care of yourself, as I have done for you, and be not over hasty how you bestow your affections. For as your fortune will be in your own hands, you will not want pretenders, and everyone will hope that you may be his prize. Your inexperienced mind," continued she, "may bring you into inconveniencies, because you'll judge of others by yourself. But now, my child, you will be left without any other defence than your own innocency, which preserve, and let virtue be your rule, and prudence guide you. Be ever deaf to rumours that detract from the honour of your friends; and if you can, warn 'em of dangers, and beware of flattery, a bait that ruins many."

I gave my dear mother a thousand thanks for her good instructions; but my grief was too great to say to her half I designed. But that very day I did resolve to acquaint her with Cleomidon and to beg her approbation; but that night — was the fatal night that robbed me of a dear mother and put a period to her life. I lost, at once, a tender mother and a wise counselor; and I may say without flattery that all her friends had a loss of her.

Thus was I left, my Indamora, in this deplorable condition, and being seized with a violent grief, I saw not the face of anyone till after her funeral rites were performed; and though I received all the consolation as was possible from Cleomidon by letters, yet it wrought but little effect upon my reason. And my mother's words ran much in my mind, that I was left without defence; for indeed I was, for I had no relations near me, only an aunt that lived beyond the Tower, and I could see her but seldom. But her young daughter she out of kindness let be with me. The poor Udotia had but dull time with me, for the melancholy I was in brought me into the yellow jaundice, that I was scarce to be known. My illness very much afflicted Cleomidon, and he showed himself very industrious in procuring me the best advice, and with his persuasions and the medicines I took, I recovered my health and looked as formerly I used to do.

I being well enough to go abroad again, Cleomidon thought he might, without any indecency, press me to a consent of marriage; for as I was absolute mistress of myself and fortune, there was no opposition on any side if I would give consent. But a humour took me that I thought in half a year, after my mother's death, I ought not to marry, and could give no other reasons for my denial. Cleomidon therefore complied with my humour, hoping that then I would (as he said) make him happy. I saw him very often; all my friends knew of his design and approved of my choice, that I may say I had all the satisfaction I could desire. But as the joys of lovers are not lasting, so did I meet with an affliction as I am certain, my Indamora, will raise your utmost compassion.

One day as Cleomidon was with me, who entertained me with news of the town, and though what he said was pleasantly related, yet I discovered a chagrin in his mind, which he seemed to take care to conceal from me; but my presaging thoughts immediately divined something there was of consequence that gave him a disturbance. And being assured I had given him no cause of jealousy or fear, I importuned him still the more to know the cause of that pensiveness that oftentimes hurried his thoughts away, that he did not sometimes answer me when I spoke to him. But he would waive the discourse, and said he did not deserve that obliging care. But then I was the more confirmed in my suspicions, and being in hopes I might dispel his grief by bearing a part with him, I forced the secret from his breast, which was, my Indamora, that Cleodora was in town. Her very name chilled my blood, I knew not why, and in my fancy rolled a thousand extravagant, ill-boding thoughts. But more was yet to come. For Alcander, Cleomidon's uncle, was in town also, and with him the most famous Lyndaraxa, Cleodora's aunt, and that their business was to make up the match with Cleomidon and Cleodora. But when he related this, he showed so much concern and trouble as cannot be imagined; and though Cleodora was to be preferred before me in several respects, yet the obliging Cleomidon told me, that if I would comply with his wishes, I should find the difference he made between us. But as I feared Alcander would not consent to his desires, so I feared he would be frustrated of his hopes forever if he disobeyed him in his marriage. But Cleomidon replied that he had rather forego all his hopes there than lose his interest in me, that since we might both live happy with our present fortunes, did beg of me not to consider his interest for the future.

I was at a nonplus what to resolve upon, that though his generous humour made him to slight his interest, yet I ought to weigh well what I did and not be the cause of so great a disappointment. 'Tis true, I was assured of his affection, and knew very well that only he could make me happy, but if he did, 'twas possible he might lose his uncle's favour forever. I had as strong a combat in my soul as ever was 'twixt love and honour, and I could not come to any resolution. That night I let him depart without any hope I would assent to his request. But the next day he came again, telling me he should be miserably unhappy if I would not promise to be his. "If," said I, "you can gain your uncle's consent, you shall not fail of mine; but if he disapproves of your ill choice, you must not disoblige him." "Madam," said he, "to lovers this is nonsense. Why should I please an uncle before myself? It is not his opinion of my happiness can make it so. But I'm the best judge in this case what will either make me happy or miserable." Cleomidon this time had like to have vanquished my obstinate humour; but being unwilling, for my sake, he should lose so considerable an estate, I urged him still to try to gain his uncle's approbation. "But, madam," said he, "what if my uncle will not consent? What destiny must I hope for?" "To marry Cleodora," said I. "Alas! Madam," replied Cleomidon, "you do not love me then, that can thus easily resign me to another? Do not flatter me any longer with vain hope, but tell me I'm become indifferent to you. Though if you will not avert my doom, there will be a necessity that I obey my uncle; and when too late, perhaps, you may repent of all your cruelty."

In justice to Cleomidon, I must acknowledge that never greater love was shown nor never worse rewarded; for he that could despise twenty thousand pound, slight his uncle's favour who had so plentiful an estate to leave him (provided he pleased him in his marriage), and yet to prefer me before Cleodora! And so insensible was I of my happiness that he could not extort a promise from me to be his, and would have married me immediately before his uncle had urged him farther. But still I continued in the same sentiments, that unless Alcander would agree to his request, I ought not to deprive him of all his hopes. But he finding me inflexible and not to be wrought upon, he took his leave of me, reproaching me with barbarity and inhumanity. But sure some magic did influence my mind, that made me so deaf to all his entreaties, that I could let him depart without one word of consolation? But I have since sufficiently repented of my cruelty.

Cleomidon that night went straight to his lodging, where he found an unwelcome guest, his uncle, who had waited for him three hours. That day Alcander by some unlucky accident had heard of our amours, and upbraided Cleomidon with it as a great mark of his folly, but desired to know the truth of that report.

But Cleomidon, who had a generous soul, scorned to deny the truth, and did frankly own to him that no other woman

77

in the world could make him happy, and that if I had pleased, he had been married to me some months since, for before he had ever known Cleodora, he had given me his heart. This free declaration put Alcander in so great a rage to see his designs opposed, that he told him, in a most imperious tone, that this was a base recompense for all his care in his education, to think of bestowing himself on any woman without his approbation. "Sir," said Cleomidon, "I ask your pardon. But our hearts are not always in our own power and by surprise sometimes are lost. There is a destiny that we cannot resist, and must sometime or other yield to love's empire." But the old gentleman, who was insensible of so soft a passion and who adored nothing but riches, was not moved but more exasperated at so dull an excuse, saying that interest ought to govern the affections, and that a wise man would look to the future and not to the present. "And," said Alcander, "I do expect that filial love and obedience from you, that you comply with my commands."

But all the reasons that Cleomidon could allege in excuse of his engagement to me, saying of me the most advantageous things that his passion could furnish him with, was of no effect, for, replied Alcander, "Has your Lindamira twenty thousand pound? Can she make you so happy as Cleodora, who has a fine house to bring you to in the country, surrounded with a good estate? And can you hope that your disobedience will be rewarded with my estate I designed to have left you when I died? Which since you can despise to gratify your love, I can bestow it on your brother, who, perhaps, will have more regard to my commands." But nothing that Cleomidon could say would mollify the obdurate heart of Alcander; for he finding that he had no inclination to obey him, he flung out of the room in a passion, threatening him with his eternal displeasure.

In such a strait never was any left, nor could anyone give higher proofs of an unalterable affection than did Cleomidon, who found my humour so refractory, that I caused him more disquiets than all his uncle's threats. But the sequel of this adventure you shall know in my next. Adieu, my Indamora.

I am your

Faithful servant,

Lindamira

Letter XIII

That night Cleomidon took but little rest, my dear Indamora, who suffered inquietudes that cannot be expressed, and
the next day recounted to me all that had passed between Alcander and himself. "That now, Lindamira," said he, "if you
refuse to make me happy, I must accuse you of too much ill-
nature and inhumanity." But instead of working that effect
on my heart as it ought, I suffered myself to be vanquished
by my generosity, and told that faithful lover that I would
rather choose to be miserable all the days of my life than he
should lose the reward of his obedience; that I would live un-
married for his sake and retire to some solitary place, where I
should never hear the name of Cleomidon; that I would not
oppose his felicity with Cleodora, for, said I, "How do I know
how your sentiments may change hereafter when I have lost
that little beauty I have, and that you once consider that for
my sake you disobliged a kind uncle?"

Cleomidon took those words mortally ill, for, said he, "They
sound not kind from the lips of Lindamira. And, madam,"
continued he, "what have you observed in my humour that
can inspire you with so mean an opinion of me? Have not I
given you all possible proof of a faithful and unalterable affection? And have not I sacrificed a considerable fortune and,
what I value more, a most kind and obliging uncle to you?
Tell me, madam, what further demonstrations you can re-

quire of my sincerity?" Though I had all imaginable reason
to be satisfied in the humour and affection of Cleomidon, yet
as our ill destinies would have it, his great merits were not
crowned with that recompense he desired. I refused absolutely
to marry him, and persuaded him to comply with his uncle.
This he resented so ill from me that, thinking I had a secret
aversion for him and that the thoughts of a near alliance disgusted me, he, sighing, said, "Well, madam, I will marry Cleodora because I see it pleases you; and if I can as well disguise
my aversion to her as you have your affection to me, I may in
time forget Lindamira, that has so ill rewarded the most constant and faithful of lovers."

This reproach extremely afflicted me, for I valued Cleomidon
beyond all things in the world; and though I ought to have
been more just to his merits, yet I could not persuade myself
he should mix his fortune with mine. This dire resolve was an
unexpressible affliction to him; and being possessed I had an
antipathy to him, he rose up to be gone, telling me he would
obey me and, as a demonstration of his love, that I should see
he would make all things easy to him when it might contribute to my satisfaction. These words were like a dagger to my
heart, that he should have such wrong notions of that friendship I had for him. I therefore endeavoured to convince him
that greater proof could not be given of a sincere affection
than to sacrifice my own quiet and happiness to his interest,
and that in persuading him to comply with his uncle was his
advantage, not mine. "Ah! Madam," saith he coldly, "you are
so much mistress of your heart and of your affections, that I
being unworthy of so great a blessing as being your husband,
I must not pretend to vanquish a resolution you have made of
rendering me forever miserable. So I will take from your sight
a person that is become detestable and odious to you."

He gave me not time to reply but made a bow and went out
of the room, fetching such sighs as would have made a heart
of stone to relent. Then I began to see my error and blame

myself for my insensibility. I sent a servant immediately after him, but for my ill fortune could not set eyes on him, for he went the quite contrary way. I gave vent to my tears, but they brought me small relief; for my ill-boding heart told me I repented too late, nor could I resolve to see him in the arms of my rival, which showed that he was not indifferent to me. I was then more sensible how unworthily I had requited so sincere an affection, which merited a better state than what he so ardently desired. The next morning I wrote to him, but the messenger brought back my own letter, which put me in a great consternation what the reason should be. But he told me that Cleomidon was gone out an hour before he went, that his man knew not where, who said that his master seemed extremely afflicted and had not slept all that night. This news gave me the most cruel and sharpest pain I ever felt, for I was conscious to myself I was the cause of that disturbance in his mind. I sent again that afternoon to his lodging, but he was not returned. But in the evening the messenger I sent met with him, who gave the letter to Cleomidon, which he read, and sighed extremely, and tears were seen to fall from his eyes, which he endeavoured to hide. "But," said he, "tell Lindamira I have not time to answer her letter, for this is my nuptial night, but she shall have a letter from me tomorrow."

Where shall I find words, my Indamora, to express my grief, my surprise, and my repentance? My passion was without moderation. I was almost drowned in my tears, I was deaf to all reason, to the persuasions of those that were with me. Nothing but the name of Cleomidon could I utter. His love was magnified in my fancy. My rival appeared, to my imagination, fair and fond of him, who was infinitely more fortunate than I, for without knowing the least uneasy thought, she possessed the most deserving man alive, and I had lost him through a foolish caprice of my own. I could blame none but myself for my ill fate; I had not this relief to think he had deserved my resentments by any neglect of his, but, on the contrary, he was faithful and generous to an infinite degree. Thus did I torment myself all that night, without letting sleep to close my eyes, though sometimes I was willing to flatter myself this was a trick to try my constancy, and by that he might find if my affection answered his. But alas! It was too true, for from a letter from Cleomidon I received a confirmation of the message he had sent, which contained these few words.

CLEOMIDON TO LINDAMIRA

I have obeyed you, madam, and am married to Cleodora; but with that reluctancy, that it had been a generous charity to have deprived me of my life when, by the rigour of your commands, I gave my hand to Cleodora. But my heart is still yours. Use it as severely as you please, for you can make no addition to my present misfortune; for I am, of all men, the most miserable, and the only comfort I can find is that I have obliged my cruel Lindamira, whom, in my heart, I must adore, whilst life remains in

Your disconsolate
Cleomidon

I read this letter with such inquietudes of mind that I knew not what I read, nor could I believe, at first, that it was the hand of Cleomidon; but by often perusing it, to my unspeakable grief, I knew my doom, and that the heart of this faithful friend belonged to another, though he told me it was still mine. It was a long time before I could resolve what answer to return. I wrote him twenty several letters before I pitched upon one I thought proper to send him, for still my pen would write so kind and so sensible of his grief, that I thought I should commit a great indiscretion if I did not alter my style; so, at last, I concluded upon this answer.

LINDAMIRA TO CLEOMIDON

I will not endeavour to excuse the rigour you accuse me of, since Cleomidon has put himself out of the power of being mine. May my wishes be propitious, and that in Cleodora you may find more happiness than you expected. Look upon her as your wife, and forget Lindamira, who merited not the happiness of being yours. But, in spite of my hard destiny, I must esteem what I once thought worthy of my love.

Adieu

To this letter he returned an answer, too kind for the husband of Cleodora but not for the lover of Lindamira, but as such I was to look upon him; therefore I concluded that I ought not to send him any more, lest it should keep up the flame I wished might be extinguished in his heart. I only then sent a message by Iris to desire him to write no more, for I would not answer any letters from him. This he resented unkindly, which, he said, was an aggravation of his grief; for he proposed some redress by receiving these innocent testimonies of my affection, but he would submit to whatever I thought fit.

At the return of Iris I was informed of the particulars of this precipitate resolution he took and executed. For when he parted from me, in his way home he encountered Alcander, who obliged him to go along with him, which was to Cleodora's lodging. When he was there, the cruel Lyndaraxa so craftily played her part as to prevail with Alcander to resolve upon the marriage the next day betwixt her niece and Cleomidon, who was then so extremely discontented at my denial, as being prepossessed with an opinion I had a secret aversion to him, that he consented to the proposal, without the least thought of having any settlements made at his marriage as Alcander had always promised him; but blindly he obeyed him the next morning, for which rash deed, he said, he never could enough repent of.

About a month after, in the same family another wedding was celebrated, which was that of Alcander with Lyndaraxa, who, by her cunning and insinuation, had so flattered the old gentleman as to persuade him to marry her; for she had deep designs in what she did. For though Alcander was of a covetous temper, yet he would have been just to his word had not Lyndaraxa influenced his mind so far as to make him forget the duty Cleomidon paid him.

At another time, this disappointment in his uncle's marriage would have been a great affliction to him. But his soul was so ruffled and disturbed at what could not be remedied, that he seemed not the least disgusted at it, but made what haste he could out of town; for in the country he could better conceal his discontents from his friends than when he was continually amongst them. I will leave him there for two years in the enjoyment of his Cleodora, who had no reason to be dissatisfied with him, for he treated her with great civility and respect. I heard by some gentlemen of that country that he was grown extreme melancholy and did not much care for company. He walked much alone, and books were his greatest entertainment.

A little before the departure of Cleomidon, you, my dear Indamora, came to town with the amiable Lucretia, from whom I have received a thousand obligations which I despair of requiting. It was through your persuasions I was induced to take that journey into Sussex with Lucretia and yourself. The agreeableness of the place so enchanted me, that 'twas with much regret I quitted such excellent conversation so soon, but you know, my aunt, Udotia's mother, sent for us up to town to be at the wedding of Doralisa, her eldest daughter, of whose virtues till that time I had not much knowledge. I must confess I was loath to go, for your seasonable counsels helped to support me under the greatest pressures I then sustained; but I saw no remedy but patience, and that difficult virtue I endeavoured to practice. The remembrance of Cleomidon was ever present in my thoughts; he appeared to me more lovely than ever; my esteem of him was equal to his virtue. I applied myself to read philosophy, but the precepts of the wise did not influence my mind at all; for I found it impossible to forget him that had loved me even to idolatry, and as great souls are most capable of a lasting passion, I did not endeavour to oppose that inclination in my heart but did resolve to love him eternally. Company was troublesome to me, and I renounced all sort of *divertissements* for the pleasure of being alone and of thinking on him. But you, my Indamora, would not suffer me to indulge myself in so great a melancholy, and you argued so well against the ill effects of thinking much, and of giving way to a fruitless repentance, that at last you made me sensible that we ought to submit to our lot, and that none were truly miserable that were not wanting to themselves.

I left you then in Sussex and came to London; my aunt received me with all the kindness imaginable. I was much charmed with Doralisa, my cousin, who had been come out of France half a year before. Her humour was very lively and taking, and her conversation the most agreeable in the world. She was something negligent in her dress, which I thought made her appear more beautiful. Her eyes are full of sweetness; her face is excellently well made, her skin of an admirable whiteness; when she speaks, she delights all that hear her; for what she says is full of wit; but above all, there is something in her voice that is full of sweetness and harmony.

You will not wonder, my Indamora, I took an affection for a relation so very deserving, who bore a part with me in all my afflictions. She made me partly forget my sorrows by her pleasant conversation. She would entertain me with the splendor and magnificence of the French king, of his amours, and of the gallantry of that nation; their politeness and acuteness in conversation; and made me an ingenuous confession of a conquest she had made of one of the greatest gallants of the court. And believing this digression will not be displeasing to you (since nothing of moment happened to me of a considerable time), I will entertain you with the adventures of my cousin, which will serve to pass away your idle intervals in the country, which will be more diverting than my own, wherein has been so long a sense of melancholy that in my next you shall have an account of her amours as faithfully as my memory can relate them.

But having finished that part you so much desired to know, and by what ill fate I became so unhappy, I have, my Indamora, given you an impartial account both of my thoughts and actions. I beg you will have some indulgence for me; and though you may justly tax me with many faults, yet I know your kindness is so generous as not to upbraid me with them, but, like a friend, will not despise the small present I have made you, which pray accept with the same goodness as you have ever done whatever fell from the pen of, my dearest Indamora,

Your most true
and faithful servant,
Lindamira

Letter XIV

When Doralisa went into France, she was in her seventeenth year. She accompanied a lady of considerable quality and of great reputation, to whose care she was committed by her parents. She had not been long in Paris but she was visited by all the English of any fashion, who were very assiduous in showing her all the diversions that mighty city afforded. Her youth and beauty soon made her be taken notice of. The French ladies took much pleasure in her company, and the bad French she at first spoke was exceeding pretty; but what by her natural sagacity, what by the influence of the best conversation, in few months she became mistress of that polite language.

As 'tis natural to love one better than another, so Doralisa found in her heart a particular esteem for a certain lady called Corinna, a very lovely person, with whom she contracted a most intimate acquaintance. In her company she passed the greatest part of her time, and Corinna being obliged to go to Fontainebleau for three months, prevailed with Doralisa to accompany her to this place. "For," said she, "it is the most delightful of any in France. It took its name originally from the fine springs that were accidentally discovered by one of the late kings of France, who was charmed at the sweetness of the situation, that he built a stately palace there which, for the magnificence of its building and fine paintings, comes not much short of any of the other royal structures. In the park, which joins to the finest of the gardens, is a fountain which is called the Star by reason of seven walks of high elms that proceed from it, which lead to several parts of the park. This place," continued Corinna, "is so romantic that it raises the curiosity of most travelers to come from Paris and further to be witnesses of what fame has made so extravagantly pleasant to them. They all agree that it exceeds the best description was ever made of it. Therefore, Doralisa," said Corinna, "you must be witness of what has given so much satisfaction to all that have seen it. But that which adds to the beauty of the place is the large forest near the town, which is so rural and withal so pleasant, that some persons prefer it to the gardens, that are cultivated by all the art imaginable." Doralisa replied that the happiness of her conversation was inducement enough to wait on her wherever she went; but she had received so perfect an idea of Fontainebleau, by the ingenious description she had given of it, that she figured to herself all that was delightful in that place. "But," said Corinna, smiling, "you will oblige me more than you imagine by the enjoyment of your company; for that is the place where I first took breath, and having sucked in that air I naturally affect it more than any place in France. Therefore resolve upon this journey, and let me know if any place in England exceeds what I shall show you there." Doralisa could not withstand her amiable friend's request, and in few days they took this pleasant journey, which was in the month of May.

The next day after their arrival these two charming ladies went to view these celebrated gardens, the grottoes, and the fountains, and Doralisa was extremely delighted with the waterworks and admired the variety of them; and within the grotto the waters fell from one basin to another, which made so melancholy a sound and yet so pleasing that she thought herself within an enchanted island, nor had she power to stir had not Corinna forced her from thence, to take a walk up to the Star-fountain, which pleased her beyond what she had seen yet — not for the beauty of the fountain, but for those seven shady walks of high elms that lead from it to several parts of the park. Upon the side of this fountain these ladies sat them down to rest themselves and to admire the excellent design of all that they had seen. "I must acknowledge," said Doralisa, "that this surpasses what I ever saw in England, and I think my time so well recompensed for the pains I have taken in walking so long, that I must do justice to Fontainebleau, and I tell you I think it the most delightful and most charming place in the world." "But you have not seen all," said Corinna, "that deserves your admiration, and that is the palace of our great monarch, which will merit your attention in viewing the curious paintings in it."

At these words they rose up and went into the first court, that leads to the front of the palace, where they beheld the noble designs of the architecture; but when they entered this magnificent building, they saw enough to admire. They passed into the galleries, where hung the pictures of the late kings and queens of France, as also the portrait of the present king, the dauphin, and dauphiness, and those of the most celebrated beauties of the court, which afforded to Doralisa a great deal of delight, who had a natural genius to painting, and had so much skill to judge of how great value they were and, being more knowing than most ladies are, could distinguish originals from copies, that her eyes were never satisfied; the more she looked, the more she admired. But the obscurity of the night coming on forced her to forsake a place that had so charmed her senses. Doralisa gave her friend a thousand thanks for the pleasures of that evening's walk; and these two charming beauties concluded upon passing most of their evenings there, but were prevented by the sudden arrival of the court of France, which was then extremely magnificent and splendid, so that Doralisa unexpectedly saw all that was rare in France and the most celebrated beauties of that time. We will sup-

pose the inhabitants of Fontainebleau full of joy for the arrival
of their monarch, and in the midst of their acclamations I'll
take leave of my dear Indamora, and am

Her most faithful
Friend and servant,
Lindamira

Letter XV

The king, who seldom honoured Fontainebleau with his royal presence, filled his people's hearts so full of joy for his arrival, that they thought they could never enough express their satisfaction; and being informed the king the next day was gone to take a walk in the park, the inhabitants flocked thither in great numbers; and to show their respect to their king, they all dressed themselves in their best apparel, and made as fine an appearance as they could. Amongst this number was Corinna and Doralisa. When coming into the park, they discovered at a distance the king and his attendants a-walking, and being led on by their curiosity, they advanced towards the fountain, where they stood to expect the king, who in another of the walks was coming that way, where they all waited for his arrival. When His Majesty was arrived at the fountain, he was pleased to make a stop to show himself to his people, who made their obedience to him, and he seemed much pleased to behold the multitude of people that was flocked thither to see him. Amongst the crowd were a great many young ladies, who had placed themselves next to the fountain to have a better view of the king, who was pleased to take a particular notice of them, for 'tis well known he is no enemy to the fair sex. And having observed them all, he at last fixed his eyes on Doralisa, and perceiving she was not a native of the place (for her complexion far exceeded any there) it excited a curiosity in him to know who she was, and turning to one of the lords of his retinue, demanded who Doralisa was and of what country. But he, not being able to satisfy His Majesty, made inquiry of some that stood by, and all the information he could get was that she was called "La Belle Angloise." The king seemed much pleased with the innocence of her looks and her modest countenance, and said to those that were near him that if the ladies of England were all so handsome as Doralisa, their conquests would exceed those of their monarch over his enemies. But the king fixed his eyes so much on her that all that perceived him looked on her to admire what took up his attention so much, which Doralisa perceiving, it made her blush, and she modestly withdrew from the company.

Corinna said a thousand pleasant things to her upon this adventure, telling her her beauty would get her enemies as well as friends, for she could assure her there was a lady at the court that would be very jealous of her did she know what notice the king took of her, which would be a secret to her no longer than till the news could be brought to her; to which Doralisa replied that her charms were not capable of raising jealousy, especially in the breasts of the French ladies, who generally had too much wit to assist themselves with what might never happen. "But tell me," said Doralisa, "when I shall see the fair Bellamira, in whose praise you have spoke so much that I am become impatient for a sight of that amiable person?" "We will go tomorrow," replied Corinna, "and I shall oblige Bellamira in bringing her so fair a visitant, and you will find her very caressing and obliging."

The next day these two agreeable friends went to pay their service to Bellamira, who received them with equal respect, and Corinna presented Doralisa to her as a person worthy of her friendship. "For," said she, "madam, this English lady is one whom I infinitely esteem and whose agreeable qualities have so endeared me to her, that I could not resolve upon this journey till I had prevailed with Doralisa to accompany me in it, which I'm certain she cannot repent of, since I've procured her the sight of the charming Bellamira, and your friendship I also desire as a recompense of the favour she has done me." To which Bellamira replied that she should readily obey her, for she found an inclination in her soul to love that charming lady; but since she was her friend, she had an obligation upon her to love what she thought worthy. Doralisa was so charmed with the obligingness of these two ladies that she wanted words to express her gratitude and sense of their favours. And after these compliments were passed, Bellamira demanded of Doralisa if she had seen the palace and the apartment of the king and dauphin. Doralisa replied that she had been over a great part of the palace, but there yet remained a larger part of this stately building she had not yet seen. "If you please then," said Bellamira, "let me have the honour to show you what remains, and I will also procure you the sight of the king's closet, wherein are rarities of an inestimable value." Doralisa readily accepted of this offer, and suffered herself to be conducted by Bellamira. This fair troop then went first to see the king's closet, which gave them cause enough for their admiration; from thence they passed through several apartments and came into the stone-gallery, which leads to the garden of orange trees. Bellamira desired them to observe how the marble stones of the gallery were discoloured with blood in several places, which the art of man could not wash out; "for the blood that is unjustly spilt," said she, "will remain to perpetuate the memory of the murderer." These words raised a curiosity in Doralisa to know the cause of it, which Bellamira acquainted her was done by the command of the queen of Swede-land to one of her own domestics whom she thought worthy of her just resentments, and caused him there to be shot to death whilst she stood by to see him executed; but the particulars of it is in print, which makes me run it over so briefly, and therefore, I believe, not unknown to yourself.

From thence they went into the garden of orange trees, where once happened a scene of mirth which Bellamira promised to acquaint them with. As soon as Doralisa had surveyed the garden and beheld in what order it was kept, and her sense of smelling so gratified with the odoriferous scents of orange flowers and jessamine, that she turned about to her two companions and told them she thought this so delicious a place, that she could resemble it to nothing so much as to Cupid's garden he prepared to entertain his fair Psyche in. "Others have been of your mind," replied Bellamira; "but, if you please, you shall see those excellent pieces of the greatest statuaries of their time," which she showed to these ladies, but made them observe a marble pedestal whereon was no statue, but had on it once one of the fairest in the world. "By what accident is it not there now?" said Doralisa.

"You must know," said Bellamira, "that one summer when the court was here, two of the ladies of the queen's bedchamber took up an humour of walking here every evening, which they spent in the admiration of those most famous artists that had made these statues you see. They pretended to have much judgment and skill in true shape and proportion, and thought they had as much knowledge as the artists themselves. This being their constant diversion in an evening, there was a young cavalier of the court who designed to play these ladies a trick, which he thus executed: one night he placed himself on the pedestal you see, in the posture of a Mercury, with his right hand extended out and his left leg raised up, as if he was upon some great expedition to the gods. Thus was he placed when these ladies passed by, and perceiving a new statue erected, they made a stop to behold what to their eyes appeared more rare than any of the others. One of the ladies, who was named Paulina, made great acclamations of wonder that anything of art could imitate nature so well and so much to the life, saying that never was a truer proportion seen, and limbs so exactly fine, and a body so exquisitely well made! 'Ah!

95

Mademoiselle,' said Lucina, 'look on this face, and there you'll
see cause for the admiration; see how much life there is in
those eyes, what a noble mien he has, how much spirit appears
through the lines of that face, which to me seems the most
charming of anything living I ever saw!' 'In fine,' said Paulina,
'I never saw anything so admirable, so delicate, and so much
to the life, as this Mercury.'

"As they were thus employed in the contemplation of their
Mercury, the spark being tired with standing so long in one
posture, he gently lets fall his leg to rest himself, which the
ladies perceiving, they thought it had been a spirit, and being
extremely surprised at this adventure, they ran away and
screeched so loud that the court was in an uproar and imagined
some person had been murdered. The spark, who apprehended
the consequences of their screeches and loud cries, leaps from
the pedestal and ran after them to convince them he was no
spirit, which they perceiving, redoubled their cries and their
speed and came running into the gallery like two furies, but
were not able to speak a word, their astonishment was so great.
In the meantime some gentlemen had the curiosity to go into
the garden to find out the cause of this outcry, which they
soon discovered by meeting the Chevalier de B—— behind an
orange tree, who was so ashamed and confounded at this unlucky accident, that of a long time he was not able to speak to
make his defence for this frolic; but his generous friends took
pity on him and caused a cloak to be brought to cover him,
and so conducted him a back way to his own apartment,
where, after he had recovered the vexation this adventure had
put him into, he gave a most pleasant relation of the praises
the ladies had given him and what excellencies they had discovered in his shape and proportion, which he recounted so
agreeable that he afforded to his friends a great deal of diversion, which they had to his cost. And after this accident nothing was talked of but the beau-Mercury. But this unhappy discovery of the Chevalier de B—— caused him much disgrace;

for the ladies were so malicious as to complain of him, that had given them so much satisfaction, and obtained of the king that he might be banished from the court, highly exaggerating the boldness of the action as being committed in His Majesty's garden. Therefore young Mercury tacitly withdrew; and in his absence his friends interceded so happily for him, that they procured his pardon of the king, and after two months' exile he returned triumphant over the causers of his disgrace. The ladies were so concerned at his good fortune that they withdrew from the court, for they could not endure the sight of him; but they repented of it afterwards, for some new adventure happened soon after which always drives the latter out of remembrance. For in courts where love and gallantry are so much practiced as in the court of France, there never wants for news."

Bellamira having finished her narration, her two charming friends returned her thanks for the entertainment she gave them, and went away very much satisfied with what they had heard and seen and, at parting, made an agreement to be at Bellamira's apartment the next evening, who had promised to procure a friend that should introduce them into the king's presence when he was at supper, for which favour Bellamira received a thousand thanks. And so they parted and betook themselves to their beds, where I will leave them to enjoy their pleasing dreams; and must hope from my Indamora's goodness a pardon for my inabilities in describing the genius of these French ladies, for the little conversation I have had with those of that nation (more than what was requisite for my learning of the language) I hope will atone for my fault, and that you will accept of this imperfect relation from

Your
Lindamira

Letter XVI

The time of assignation being come, Doralisa and Corinna went to the apartment of Bellamira, who impatiently waited their arrival and, embracing them both, "My charming friends," said she, "none but yourselves can judge what inquietudes I have suffered in your absence; that if I am as far advanced in your esteem as you are both in mine, you may apprehend what 'tis to be separated from those one loves." Her two friends replied that their sentiments were the same, and had come sooner than the appointed hour, had not company prevented them. Soon after, came in the Marquis of L——, who was allied to Bellamira, and from him expected the conduct of these ladies to the palace of the king. The young marquis testified, both by his words and actions, how great an honour it was to him. After some discourse of indifferent things, they fell upon that of love and gallantry. The marquis, who was the most accomplished man in the court and was naturally very amorous, said many pleasant things upon this subject. His nature was brisk, airy, and facetious. For his fluent, natural, easy wit he was called the young Ovid, and was known more by that name than by his title. He had an admirable genius to poetry, and his compositions of that kind were of so happy, so polite, so peculiar a character, and withal so excellent a judgment, that few could equal him; and Bellamira, who knowing his admirable talent that way, entreated him to repeat some of his verses to her two amiable friends, which the marquis modestly refused at first; but seeing the ladies would be obeyed, he repeated some verses in imitation of Virgil, which he performed with an admirable grace; and Corinna (who never yet discovered her genius that way) gave him such praises that let the whole company see her wit and judgment. And finding she was very conversant in all sorts of poetry, he desired the honour of hearing some of hers and used so much impressment, that Corinna could not refuse the marquis what he desired, and repeated to him a copy of verses upon the tyranny of love and another upon jealousy, wherein she discovered much delicacy of thought; the style was noble, lofty, and natural.

Thus did these two wits entertain the company; and Doralisa told Corinna she never knew she had a faculty that way, and asked her most obligingly why she never entertained her with some of her poetry, for she was a great lover of it. She gave her this reason, that she durst never indulge the humour of versifying for fear of the censure that attends poets, who are supposed to attribute a power to mortals that belongs only to the divinity, especially when they pay incense to the fair ones they adore.

"Ah! Madam," said Ovid, "how great a solecism would it be both in a lover and a poet if he did not look upon his mistress as the sublimest object of his thoughts! And they that declaim against love or his power are not worthy to know it; and there is even a pleasure in those disquieting amours that are so much complained of; and the honour of being captivated by a lady of wit and bearing the glorious title of her servant does sufficiently recompense the disquiets that her rigour sometimes causes, since one smile or a kind look restores the lover to his former tranquillity of mind." "You speak so feelingly," said Bellamira, "as if you had experienced the rigour of some fair one; but 'tis not to be doubted but that she has repented of her too great severity, since you can so well describe the joys that one smile can give." "I cannot deny, madam," said Ovid, "but that I have known the joys, the raptures, the hopes and fears, and all the passions that attend a lover, by my own experience; and yet I do not wish to have my heart free from the torments of love, for love has something of pleasure in it: 'tis the soul of life; it quickens the apprehension, makes a man lively, brisk, and airy, notwithstanding the uneasy intervals that wait on it; and, charming Corinna," said he, turning towards her, "I am in love with your poetry, with Doralisa's modesty, and with Bellamira's great bounty in suffering so long my conversation, and being all ladies of wit and beauty, I know not on which to fix my heart. But if you would give me leave to love you all, I would be a constant admirer and confine my love to the narrow limits of three." "You give such a pleasant description of the inconstancy of your humour," replied Bellamira, "that 'tis no glory to be the mistress of Ovid, though it must be a satisfaction to be loved by a person of so much wit; and if these ladies can content themselves with part of your heart, I'll be content to divide with them." "For my part," said Corinna, "I fear I shall be jealous of my two fair rivals, that they will go away with the greatest share of it." "And I had rather have no part at all," said Doralisa and smiled, "than share it with two such dangerous rivals, which I can as ill bear in my love as a monarch on his throne. Therefore I will excuse the marquis from being in love with me, or of making any songs or verses on me, being a theme not worthy of so great a wit." "You wrong your judgment, madam," replied Ovid, "for what theme can be more sublime than that of the fair? And since I love to be sincere, I find an inclination in my soul most to be yours." " 'Tis then in oppostion to those ladies' virtues," said Doralisa, "or to the humour I have not to accept of a heart by halves." "You shall then have all," said Ovid, jocosely. "If these ladies will render back what they have in their power and so show what power your beauty can produce, you shall reign sovereign in my heart, till such time that you are tired with the sovereignty or I with your arbitrary power."

These ladies made themselves exceeding merry at the indifferent humour of the marquis, and rallied him so wittily that he was almost at a nonplus how to defend himself against their attacks; but he told them they were all so charming, so amiable, and so agreeable that if he did not depart from them, he should not have one bit of his heart left to throw at the next fair one he met; but if they would accept of it amongst them, it should be at their service. They all thanked him for the nobleness of the present, but he being so indifferent on whom he bestowed it, they thought he had best keep the jewel for his own wearing. At this the marquis rose up and was going away with a small fragment of his heart, when Bellamira reproached him with what he had promised the ladies, who had undertaken to conduct them into the king's presence, but he excused his ill memory and begged their pardon that he should forget to pay them that service he came to render them. It being time to be gone, he led this fair troop to the king's apartment and placed Doralisa where she might have the best sight of this great monarch. The king no sooner cast his eyes on her, but he remembered he had seen her at the Star-fountain; and she being a stranger at the place, His Majesty in a great compliment presented her with a plate of the finest sweetmeats there, which particular favour was received with a very graceful action from Doralisa, and her beauty was then more taken notice of than before. And that day proved a day of great conquests, which procured her the envy of some of the greatest beauties of the court.

As soon as supper was ended, these ladies retired to Corinna's apartment, where they spent the rest of the evening in relating what they had seen, and the honour the king did Doralisa was subject enough for discourse. But all on a sudden the marquis became very dull and pensive; and Bellamira demanding the cause of so great an alteration, he with a terrible sigh replied that he was become the most amorous man in the world, and did believe not any loved with so violent a passion as himself; for he was already jealous, fearful, and mistrustful.

These ladies diverted themselves at his discourse and told him his serious humour did not become him so well as his indifferent one. "But," said the marquis, turning towards Doralisa, "do you believe, madam, that a man loaded with chains can walk, speak, or look with that freedom as when his shackles were off? No, my charming fair," continued he, "you have not only fettered me but involved me in such a labyrinth of love, that I know not when I shall be able to unwind myself and get my freedom again; for I already find I would not shake off your fetters and had rather die than cure my mind, and all the frightful visions of love, of despairs and jealousies cannot divert my thoughts of being eternally yours." The marquis spoke this so seriously that all the company laughed at him and begged of him to put off his disguise and become the same pleasant Ovid he was a few hours before, and not the dull lover, which did not suit his pleasant humour; but he only answered them with sighs and became so altered that they feared he was become a lover indeed. And Bellamira, finding he could not assume his former pleasant humour, took leave of the company, and the marquis conducted her to her apartment; but had agreed before they parted to meet the next evening at the Star, from thence to take what walks suited best with their inclination. Thus did this fair company separate, as night always parts good friends, and at their next meeting you shall hear more of

Your real friend
and servant,
Lindamira

Letter XVII

The next evening the marquis was the first that appeared at the fountain, where he attended the arrival of this fair troop; but Doralisa had so wholly taken up his thoughts that he neglected answering a small billet before he parted from his lodging. He being there all alone and in a place so proper to entertain his thoughts and vent his sighs, did often repeat the name of Doralisa. "Oh, my adorable maid," said he, "my charming beauty, were I so blessed to be beloved by thee, my heart would have a joy too great to receive increase! But how can I hope to mollify a heart already (perhaps) prepossessed with some violent passion? Have I not shown that indifference to her that will give her an opinion I am incapable of love? And she will think so poorly of my love that I shall want a thousand oaths and vows to confirm her in what I say. But why I know not, my soul is so perplexed with jealousies and fears that I already suffer a martyrdom. She seems to me so wondrous fair, so full of charms and innocence, that in my extravagance of love I shall grow troublesome and dread every look she gives another."

Thus was the marquis entertaining of himself when he was surprised by Bellamira, who was the next arrived, and overhearing some broken speeches and seeing a disorder in his looks, confirmed her in the belief that he was really become amorous of Doralisa; and accosting him with a smile, "Well,

Monsieur le Marquis," said she, "I am of opinion you are become the slave of Doralisa instead of the lover of us all three. What, are your sentiments changed already? And have you forgot you throwed your heart at us all? And must Doralisa be the Venus that must go away with the prize? And must the French beauties yield to the English one? No, no," continued Bellamira, "we shall begin a quarrel with you and call your judgment in question." These latter words she spoke with so serious an air that the marquis seemed much concerned he had disobliged so amiable a friend as Bellamira, for whom he had a great esteem and friendship, and was about to make his peace with her when she prevented him, in saying that she only rallied him, and that she must allow his judgment unquestionable, since he had preferred Doralisa's beauty before hers or Corinna's. The marquis seemed overjoyed to find her sentiments so obliging, and he freely acknowledged to her that he adored that charming lady, and petitioned her assistance in the accomplishment of his happiness, which Bellamira promised to the utmost of her power. And soon after an opportunity offered itself, for the other two were far advanced into the walk before they were perceived. "Come, Monsieur," said Bellamira, "let us go meet your adorable Doralisa, and let her know, from your own mouth, how great a miracle is wrought in her favour beyond us all, that she has made a slave of the most gallant and most accomplished man in our court."

The encounter of this hero with Doralisa seemed extreme pleasant to the other two; for as formerly there appeared a joy in his eyes, a tranquillity in his mind, he became chagrin and melancholy, and his serious looks sat so ill upon him that Doralisa pleasantly reproached him for the strange metamorphosis of his soul and wished him to assume his former gayety. "For," said she, "you cannot be good company with that dismal countenance you have so affected." "Did you but know," said Bellamira, "the agitations of his soul, you would not thus rally your slave; for the marquis has made me the confidant of his passion, and you, fair Doralisa, have robbed us of our hopes." The marquis added to these words all that a violent passion could inspire him, and spoke so seriously and used such enforcing arguments, that Doralisa was forced to yield to her reason in this opinion, that he had a real affection for her. She received the marks of his esteem as an honour to her and, in the most obliging terms imaginable, returned her acknowledgment. But our lover told her he would have her alter the word acknowledgment to one more ravishing and more sublime. "What is that," said Doralisa, "that can be more pleasing?" "'Tis love, madam," replied the marquis, "and that musical sound would ravish my soul, to have it spoke by so fair a mouth as Doralisa's!" They continued walking and discoursing thus for an hour; and the marquis, who had a wit the most refined of any man living, said so many endearing and passionate things to Doralisa that she at last yielded he should own his passion for her. "For," said he, "madam, I not only make you a present of my heart, but I will not conceal the least thing in it, for I think it a treason in love not to be pardoned, to hide from the person loved whatever they know or think."

This evening seemed to the marquis the most delightful of any in his life; and though he was become a prisoner of love, his chains were not heavy to him, for he enjoyed all the satisfaction imaginable. He loved a person infinitely charming, was fair and virtuous; she used him with respect, and he had hopes that she one day might be his, for he had a fortune to make her happy, but as yet only begged leave to adore her. For two months did he pass his time in the agreeable conversation of these ladies, and received from Doralisa a confirmation of her esteem and friendship.

But as the joys of lovers are not lasting, so it proved to the poor marquis, who according to his usual custom attended the king's levee, and one morning, as soon as His Majesty was dressed, he retired into his closet and commanded the marquis to follow him. As soon as he appeared, the king in a very obliging manner told him that he designed to make him Lieutenant General of his forces, and that he must prepare to depart in ten days, and added that he knew none in his court that could acquit themselves so well as himself, for both his courage and fidelity had been tried. This news was like a thunderbolt to his heart, but he dissembled his trouble as well as possible he could and gave His Majesty thanks for the honour he did him; and though it was with reluctancy he accepted this commission, yet durst he not refuse it. The marquis made his obeisance to the king and went straight to Bellamira to communicate to that charming friend his griefs and vexations.

He complained to her of the severity of his destiny. "For," said he, "I never knew how to love till now. I have made a mock of that blind deity and defied his power, but now I find he has revenged himself of my insensibility, and I am forced to depart from her that has possessed my heart, my soul, and all my thoughts." Bellamira heard his complaints with much sorrow, for she had a real esteem for him. "What think you, Monsieur le Marquis?" said she. "Have you not some enemies at court that have thought of this expedient to remove you from His Majesty?" "No, no, Bellamira," said he, "no enemies would seek my preferment; but 'tis only to His Majesty that I am indebted for this honour, who doubtless admires the fair Doralisa and is become my rival." "These surmises of yours," said Bellamira, "are ill-grounded, and he may admire the beauty of Doralisa and not love her. But confess the truth," continued she and smiled. "Have you not writ verses and panegyrics on the beauty of the fair Honoria? And have you not entertained her after so gallant a manner as to persuade her you were in love with her?" " 'Tis true," said Ovid, "I have professed much gallantry in all my actions, and was kind to her, as I was to the rest of the fair sex; but I am certain, I never loved any but Doralisa; but what does this import to my departure, charming Bellamira?" "O! very much," replied she, "for this incensed beauty is become jealous of Doralisa, and, to my knowledge, is grown very melancholy since you have owned your love to the fair one you adore, that she is hardly knowable. She converses with very few; and her most intimate friend is Angellina, who, you know, has a great power with the king. With her she sometimes spends whole evenings, when her royal lover is not there; and my opinion is, that she, despairing of a happiness you would bestow on Doralisa, has bethought herself of this revenge, that her rival may be as miserable as herself, if possible." "That cannot be," said the marquis, "if Doralisa can but love like me; though long absences are hard to bear, yet if a mistress loves, and is sincere, faithful, and constant, the hopes of seeing her again makes one endure a thousand other misfortunes, and does excite courage in a man that he may do a brave action, worthy of the honour of being her slave. But to bear this separation, I stand in need of all my courage, fortune, and patience." But after a long and fruitless complaint, the marquis left Bellamira, and went to seek his consolation in the sweet conversation of Doralisa and Corinna, to whom he related this news, which extremely surprised and grieved them both. And till this accident, Doralisa did not think she had more than esteem and friendship for the marquis; which he perceiving, "Ah, my adorable Doralisa," said he, "am I so happy to have you partake in my sorrows? Can a beauty, so divine, mix her griefs with mine? This is ravishing beyond all my hopes, and yet it is but justice my Doralisa should sympathize with me, that pay her so awful an adoration." Doralisa then did no longer scruple to own the perplexity of her soul, and told the marquis that she should suffer no less than he in this cruel absence; but the esteem she had for him she would preserve entirely, or till such time that he had forgot her; but these words drew from his mouth a thousand imprecations and vows of eternal fidelity.

But during this short time the marquis had at Fontainebleau, he dedicated all his time to Doralisa, and neglected some
business of importance; but so much she did employ his
thoughts, that this fair one reigned sole empress in his heart.
All the evenings were generally passed away in the park or
gardens in the company of his adored mistress and her agreeable companions, where he would bid a thousand adieus to
those conscious scenes of his most faithful love. To the trees,
rocks, and fountains did he bid an eternal farewell, that sometimes one would think that love had quite distracted him. The
time of his separation drew near, and he had but two nights
more to pass at Fontainebleau when, one evening, as he was in
company of these charming ladies, a page presented him with
a letter, saying he waited his answer. The marquis, retreating
two or three steps, opened the letter and found these words:

I am driven to the last extremity, that am forced to tell the
insensible marquis I love him a thousand times more than my
own soul; and 'twere a blessing to me to be deprived of this
wretched life, that I could no longer see the happiness of my
rival. How many times have I seen you walking with her, and
whispering to her all the kind things your passion could inspire? Judge then how it wracks my soul to behold her felicity,
whilst I, poor miserable I, have no redress but to my tears. Return, return, ungrateful man, and render back that heart that
only belongs to me; for it was first given to me, and in ex-
change I gave you mine! Say that it was my own precipitate
inclination that seduced me, yet it was your good humour that
charmed me; and what is the effects of this but sighs and tears
and tormenting disquiets, nay, and the worst of deaths, a jealousy insupportable! Adieu.

Honoria

This letter gave the marquis great disturbance; but he called
up all his courage, and turning to the page, told him he would
wait on Honoria. After this dispatch, he made up to the ladies,

who expected his return, and Doralisa expressed great inquietudes, fearing it was a challenge he had received (though she
apprehended none upon her own account), but he being so
general an admirer of the sex, she knew not what to imagine,
and asked him most obligingly if it was good news. "No, bad,"
said the marquis, and smiled, "for the fair ones are too good-
natured to hurt those that pay them that respect their merits
claim from us." "What do you mean by these words?" said
Bellamira. "Has Honoria sent you that billet?" "Why do you
guess Honoria?" said the marquis. "For those reasons I have
formerly told you," replied Bellamira, "and therefore conceal
no longer from us what is no secret." And being overcome by
their entreaty, he promised to show the letter, provided they
would not speak of it; for he thought it beneath a man of honour to boast of favours from the fair sex. They all promised
him secrecy, and then produced this letter that so much afflicted him, not being in a capacity of retaliating the kindness
Honoria expressed for him; he presented the letter to Doralisa, saying that he never imagined his indifferent way of making love to Honoria would have produced these effects, for he
did believe she had wit enough to take all in raillery he had
said; for though he thought her fair, witty, and agreeable, he
n'ere had more than esteem for her. But Doralisa reproached
him with the inconstancy of his humour and told him, the
next new face he saw would drive her out of his remembrance,
and that she must expect the same fate of Honoria, to whom
she thought he ought to go and make his peace before his departure; but she spoke this in such a tone, that let the marquis
see he was not indifferent to her, which extorted from him
vows of fidelity, and that his never-dying passion should continue to the last period of his life. However, this adventure
gave him so much disturbance, that he stood in need of all his
courage to bear up his great heart against the reproaches of a
lady of Honoria's humour; but being commanded by Doralisa
to wait on her, he left this agreeable company in the garden

to go to one whom he had a mortal aversion for. But the melancholy that appeared in Doralisa's eyes testified to her two fair companions that the marquis was the cause of it, and that the hazards of war made her to apprehend much danger for him; but she received from these ladies all the consolation she was capable of.

And whilst they entertained themselves on this subject, the disconsolate Honoria had before her eyes nothing but despairs and jealousies; and the cruel thoughts of the insensible Ovid filled her fond soul with so much grief, that she often called on that kind tyrant death to take her from her restless bed; or that her faithless charmer would come posting to her, and bring her the welcome tidings of his eternal love. Whilst thus her thoughts were busied with his ingratitude, the unhappy marquis entered her chamber; with disorder, both in his looks and steps, approached this incensed beauty, who was so buried in her grief that she heard him not till he had approached her bed. The sight of him awakened in her all her just resentment (for she thought herself dishonoured to be abandoned for Doralisa), that anger took place of her love, and she rose up from off her bed, and darting flashes of anger from her eyes, "Are you come," said she, "to reproach my weakness, for having too much love for an insensible and ungrateful man? Or are you come to tell me you will abandon Doralisa for me?" "Madam," said the marquis, "I come in obedience to your commands, not to reproach the fair, nor to tell you I can alter my sentiments for Doralisa." She hardly gave him leave to bring out these words, but reassuming a fierce look and a shrill voice, she told him that his insensibility should be rewarded, and that he should find the effects of her indignation. The marquis was about to justify his conduct to her, and that it was only gallantry he had professed. She multiplied words so fast upon him, that no cannon shot in the besieging of a city could fall with more impetuosity than did her reproaches upon the marquis. She thundered in his ears and stormed about the room like one distracted, that though the marquis wanted not for courage and was as valiant as any man, yet did he not know how to defend himself against her assaults and batteries; but being resolved not to retreat till the danger was over, he expected with patience the result of this hurricane; and when Honoria had said all the bitter things her anger could suggest, she let fall a shower of tears, which would have mollified the heart of any other than the marquis, whose soul was entirely fixed on the invincible charms of Doralisa, whose treatment to the marquis was always mild and full of sweetness. When he saw she was in a condition of heark'ning to him, he grieved his hard fate that he knew not sooner those generous sentiments she had honoured him with, that now he was not in a condition to retaliate love for love.

Honoria, who was of a high spirit, could hardly bear this declaration; but, being sensible her anger would not make a lover break his chains, she repented herself of her folly; and being out of hopes of making him of the number of her admirers, she told him it was her that had procured his commission of the king, for she found some consolation in knowing that her rival must suffer inquietudes no less than herself; "for to be absent," said she, with a malicious smile, "from the person loved will be as insupportable as the slights from those one loves." The marquis hearkened to her reproaches, her complaints, and her wishes for his ill success in war, and that the god of love would sometimes punish him for his ingratitude to her. She rose up, and went into her closet, and locked the door after her.

The marquis, who was not sorry for her abrupt departure, bid her adieu through the door, and came immediately to his beloved Doralisa, to whom he recounted all that was passed, and upon this occasion said to Doralisa the most moving, the most passionate things, that his love could inspire him with; and the malice of Honoria, in procuring his preferment, he lamented in such terms that Doralisa might see he had for her a most tender affection. The marquis offered to marry Doralisa, in hopes it might defer his departure, or that he might remit his employment to his brother; but Doralisa, who was very discreet, only testified her acknowledgments for the honour he would do her, but that she was under the command of a father and mother, and could not dispose of herself without their approbation, but she would always preserve in her heart a most real affection for him. It growing late, the marquis took leave of Doralisa, and left her in no less grief than himself for his departure. That night he gave all orders necessary for his equipage, and betook himself to his bed, where his restless thoughts would not let him take much rest; he there gave vent to his sighs, uttering the most bitter complaints that a soul, seized with so much love, could say. He sometimes cursed the malice of Honoria, and sometimes wished that Doralisa were unfaithful, and like one frantic, would say a thousand extravagant things, all that his love and rage could suggest to his fancy. Thus did he rave and sigh and turn himself a thousand times; and after all he must resolve to leave his better part, his Doralisa, behind!

The next day, as soon as it was proper to wait on his three amiable friends, he went to take his leave of them, who all lamented this separation; but Doralisa's tears expressed how great her concern was above the others. The marquis, who had a most passionate soul, was deeply touched with the marks of Doralisa's affection to him. "But," said this fair afflicted one, "is it not possible for you to forget your Doralisa in the midst of your triumphs and acclamations of joy for your victories? And will not absence work that effect, that your reason has not yet done?" "No, no, madam," said the marquis. "Fear nothing from a man who is become constant for your sake, and whose greatest glory is to wear your chains." They promised each other to write and freely to impart their thoughts. Upon these terms did these lovers part; and the absence of the marquis was a very great affliction to them all, for whether he was merry or whether he was sad, his conversation was extreme delightful.

The next day the marquis with his equipage departed from

Fontainebleau, where Doralisa remained, full of discontent for the absence of her lover. Her two friends endeavoured to divert the chagrin that appeared in her countenance, and left nothing unsaid that could give her any consolation. They continued their humour of walking whilst they remained at Fontainebleau; but Corinna, who thought that Doralisa would be more diverted at Paris, proposed going the next week; and Bellamira being so obliging to accompany them in this journey, they resolved in few days to be gone. By the first post Doralisa received a letter from the marquis, who gave her all the hopes imaginable of his fidelity; they continued their correspondence during the time she stayed in Paris, which was six months. He told her in his last that he would follow her into England, and demand her of her father and mother in marriage; but whether her answer miscarried or he changed his sentiments, I know not; but she never heard more from him. But her father, who had provided her a husband who was a gentleman of a good estate, and one who might make her happy — she, at last, consented to her parents' commands after she had expected half a year to hear news from her faithless Ovid; therefore she resolved to obey them. And it was to her wedding, my dear Indamora, I went when I left Lucretia and yourself in Sussex.

This is the account that Doralisa gave me of her adventures; if I have related them wrong, impute it to the defect of my memory. And to deal plainly with you, I am so sensible I have acquitted myself ill in this undertaking, that I could never hope for a pardon but from so generous a friend as yourself. Her amours have lost great part of their beauty by the disadvantage they have received in being penned in so unaccurate an order; but at present I shall trouble your patience with no more apologies but shall abruptly take leave of my Indamora, and am

Her faithful
Lindamira

Letter XVIII

To resume my discourse, my dearest Indamora, I must begin from the marriage of Doralisa, who stayed with my aunt about two months, and then Lysidas, her husband, took her a house near St. James's, which had belonging to it a little garden that looked into the park, which made the house extreme agreeable and pleasant. The affection Doralisa had for me and the compassion she took for that melancholy air she observed in my looks (which I could not always hide) obliged her to this great civility of inviting me to be with her, in hopes it might divert my thoughts from Cleomidon. I readily accepted her kind offer, and having liberty of complaining to her of my unhappiness, I often took the freedom to reflect on the severity of my destiny, and, as all unhappy people do, thought no misfortune like my own. But at last I took a resolution to act the part of a philosopher, to be content with my condition and not repine at what I could not help; and having brought my mind to this sedate temperament, I enjoyed much satisfaction in the conversation of Doralisa and Lysidas, who was of a very facetious humour. What diversions the town afforded, I had my share in a very moderate way; for Lysidas had an inclination to be more abroad than at home, and was not pleased unless Doralisa and I were with him; and as he had a great many visits to make to his relations, who had been with him to congratulate his ·happiness, we went very often abroad for a month or two.

But one visit amongst the rest I should have been very glad, could I been excused from making it with Doralisa; but she not knowing my reasons, which I was loath to tell her, I put it to the venture, and accompanied her to the house of Colonel Harnando. You must know his lady was near related to Lysidas, and Doralisa had some particular reasons upon the account of alliance as well as inclination to visit Elvira, who was adorned with much beauty; her wit was quick and and apprehensive, her humour always equal and full of sweetness, that I found myself charmed in her conversation, and could not but admire at the Colonel for his volatile humour. But such is the humour of most men, that they value not a treasure they are possessed of. But had not Elvira been a person of much discretion, his humour of gallantry to the ladies would have made her very uneasy. But she told a friend (as I have heard since) that to be out of humour was not the way to reduce a heart that would sometimes go astray; but his own experience of the fickleness of some women would soonest bring him back and convince him that she had sentiments more tender and more sincere, than those ladies he loved to fool his time away with; but as she had a most true and real affection for him, she was mistress enough of her resentments not to be carried to the smallest action against her duty.

Elvira very obligingly invited us to come often to her house, saying she seldom went abroad (for she was then with child) and would take it as a favour if we would bring our works along with us; to which civil request we consented, and went to visit Elvira more than any relation that Lysidas had. And my fears being over that the Colonel should know me or have any suspicion of me, I went with great freedom to his house; but he had not forgot he had seen me with Valeria and Silvanus in the park, and would often make inquiry after their healths. He was extreme obliging and complaisant, which I feared might give offence to Elvira; but she was of a contrary humour, and being very discreet, she seemed pleased with whatever the Colonel did. And that which was most strange, she grew infinitely fond of me, and would be sending continually for me to play at cards with her if she had no company; so that at last either Doralisa, myself, or both, were there three times in a week, and were very merry at our play.

But sometimes we were interrupted by troublesome visitors. As there is company of all sorts, there were fewest of the number of generous persons, and amongst the rest, one impertinent lady, who in her younger days had had beauty enough to engage hearts into an affection. These conquests raised her vanity to that degree, that she thought she merited all the praises that flattery could invent, and all her discourse was of herself, what was said to her, and what were her witty repartees again; that being so full of the thoughts of her quondam lovers, she would begin a relation of them all at once and so confound one thing with another that there was no coherence in all her discourse; yet would she oblige us to hearken to her, and take it very ill if great attention was not given. And sometimes when we were very earnest at our play, she would come in and interrupt us; she was not so complaisant as to play a game with us, but protested against it and represented to us how ill we passed our time, saying that the conversation of ingenious persons was more profitable to us. But Elvira replied that we only passed a few hours this way because we had no news to entertain ourselves with, and to talk of our neighbours and their management of their affairs was not suitable to our genius. To this the venerable old lady replied that she would divert us with the history of her life if we would leave our cards, which was immediately done. But if it were to gain a million of gold, it is impossible for me to remember the least fragments of her discourse where nine words of sense hung together. But to conclude before I begin, she was loved, slighted, hated, loved, despised, and loved again, and all in a quarter of an hour. And, I suppose, this is the very lady you have heard on, so celebrated for the prodigious conquests her eyes had made, who would entertain all people with these stories; but they must have better memories than I have, who can relate any one of them again.

But to make up the misfortune of her impertinence, amongst other visitors was a young lady of an admirable wit and pleasing conversation, who was very courteous and obliging. She happened to be that day with Elvira when this lady came to visit her, so did partake in the relation of her amours; but certainly never did anyone divert themselves so much as Clarinta did with the old lady. She would ask her so many particulars of the sparks her lovers, and put her upon the description of their persons and their humours, and her own barbarity to them she much condemned; but the old lady, to justify her conduct, would let fall words that let us see that her lovers were treated very kindly, and her fondness, we believed, was the occasion of her losing them so fast, which Clarinta took great notice of, and rallied the old lady very much, that I believe this venerable piece wished she had not been so prodigal of her words, but her gestures did more express her thoughts than her rhetoric. But, to our relief, came in the Colonel, to whom Clarinta said she wished he had come sooner, to have heard a most delightful relation of that lady's amours. The Colonel, who was naturally complaisant and full of gallantry, entreated the lady to relate all that had been said before, who was proud to obey him and transported to find him inclined to hearken unto her, which made her not omit the least circumstance to embellish her story. And the Colonel, who had that illuminated wit that is capable of all things and would sometimes be pleasantly malicious, on this occasion said so many satirical things and made so many remarks, that the whole company was diverted with him, and the lady well pleased at the mirth her folly created.

I have insisted too long upon this subject, my dear Indamora, being it defers the recital of what relates to Cleomidon, for whom you have so much concern, that I will give you the satisfaction you desire as soon as possible; but I must finish this day's adventure before I can proceed. In a short time the lady went away, and Elvira, Clarinta, Doralisa, and myself went to take a walk in the park, when unexpectedly we encountered Sir Formal Trifle with a young wench in a mask. These ladies had not ever been acquainted with his character, or had known he had ever been my lover; that if they pleased, I would give them a relation of his courtship, which was both comical and uncommon, if they were not already tired out with an account of love matters. But they complimented me so far to tell me, they should be extremely well diverted with anything I would relate to them, which I did as I have already done to you. The novelty of this Sir Formal pleased them beyond measure, which made Clarinta have a great desire to advance towards him, which she did with Doralisa whilst Elvira and I stayed behind some paces to observe them.

In the meantime, Sir Formal got rid of his masked lady; and my two friends placed themselves on the bench in the dark walk, where they expected the return of Sir Formal, who soon after walked his Spaniard's pace towards them. He observing them both to be handsome, he placed himself by them, and, in a minute, began a discourse; and Clarinta, who had an insinuating wit, soon gained his esteem and put him upon the relation of his amours, saying, some time after, she heard he had been ill treated by a young gentlewoman called Lindamira, at whose name the old knight blushed for anger, that it should be reported he had been unkindly used; and, to mention his true character, told Clarinta that he had forsaken her because she had not a fortune equivalent to his; and that he might have married her if he had pleased. But my two friends were so enraged at his vanity that they told him they knew Lindamira too well to question her judgment, or to think she would marry a man of his age and of his infirmities (for, you may remember, he was paralytic). At these words, they rose up, for they durst not stand the brunt of his anger, and left him to chew the cud.

This adventure contributed much to that evening's diversion; and Elvira told the Colonel, when she came home, that Sir Formal had been a pretender to me and asked him how he approved of such a match for me; but his eyes as well as his words told me that I deserved a better fate. And all supper-time were very merry about him; and the Colonel said a thousand pleasant things of his formality and rhetoric, for he had often been in his company, and was no stranger to his vain humour of commending himself, and was as well able to judge as anyone how little he deserved his own praises.

At last Doralisa and I took leave of our good company. What happened at my return home you shall know in my next, which will as much surprise you as it did me. I am,

My dearest Indamora,

Your friend and servant,

Lindamira

Letter XIX

I shall now acquaint you, my dearest Indamora, how pleasantly I was surprised that night I went from Elvira, when on my toilette, as I was undressing me, I cast my eye on a letter whose characters I knew to be that of Cleomidon. I took it up, and turned it forty ways before I had power to open it; and Iris, who observed the different agitations of my mind, asked me if I had not courage to open a letter from Cleomidon. "No, Iris," said I, "for I cannot imagine why he should write to me, since hitherto he has so religiously observed my commands." "It may import some good news," replied Iris; "and I beseech you, madam, read what Cleomidon has sent you." At her importunity at last I opened it, and the contents of this letter struck me with great astonishment; for he acquainted me that Cleodora was no longer amongst the living, and that being at liberty to dispose of himself, he hoped I would admit him to lay his life and fortune at my feet, making it his earnest request that no capricious fancies or needless formalities might retard or hinder his happiness, if I still preserved an esteem for him, and lastly, that as soon as he could settle his affairs, he would come to town. I leave you to judge, my Indamora, if my grief was great for Cleodora; but yet I was in no transport of joy, for I knew he was in some trouble for her death.

I writ to Cleomidon, and scrupled not to own that neither time nor absence had defaced the impression he had made, and had entirely preserved my affections for him; the hopes of seeing him soon made me less copious in my expressions of that esteem I had for him. In a short time I received an answer to that, which testified his impatience of seeing me; that as soon as a month was expired, he would wait on me. I then began to think myself in a state of happiness, since I was beloved by the most virtuous and most constant of lovers, and that Cleomidon was in a capacity of owning it to all the world.

But before the arrival of my generous Cleomidon, I must not omit to give you the character of the young Octavius, a nephew of Lysidas, who made frequent visits to his house. His person was well made, genteel, and handsome; but there ever appeared a disturbedness in his eyes, which was the effects of an unbridled jealousy; and, in a few days, was grown all melancholy and sullen. But 'tis the nature of jealousy to force an interpretation of all things to their own disadvantage. Octavius was fallen desperately in love with a young lady of a good fortune, who had for him a great esteem and always used him with great respect, and those innocent favours she showed him would have made another lover (that was not of his humour) think himself very happy. But on the contrary, Octavius became jealous of Belisa because she was favourable to him; and being prepossessed that all men were treated like himself, he grew mistrustful and pettish and employed himself in observing all the actions of Belisa, who was a person very charming and agreeable; though not a celebrated beauty, yet one who had an obligingness in her countenance that all that see her were pleased with her.

Octavius often coming to Lysidas, I observed this change in him and was curious to know the cause of it; for I know he was esteemed very much by Belisa, that I could not imagine the occasion of this chagrin. He told me that never man suffered so much for love as he did; for his jealousy was so great, that he found no consolation in what was past nor in the present nor in what was to come.

I would not flatter him so much to tell him he deserved the

pity of any rational creature. For I would sooner marry a man that hated me than one that loved me with jealousy; for no torment was like the jealousy of an imperious husband, for that passion would seduce their reason, trouble their senses, and make them find more than they seek for. But Octavius would maintain that love and jealousy were inseparable. Our opinions were fire and water, and could not alter each other's sentiments upon the matter.

I represented to him the injustice he did Belisa, being jealous without a cause, especially since he found it so tyrannical a passion, and that it ran him into so many misfortunes; but the jealous Octavius said he would still love Belisa and still be jealous. His obstinate humour would sometimes vex me and sometimes divert me, but all the precepts and examples I could offer wrought no effect on him; till one day he came to make me a visit, and was saying he was still the most unhappiest of lovers; for when he was out of Belisa's sight, he fancied she was beset with rivals and that she was kind to all and that her reservedness was only an affected humour, that she suffered his courtship only in obedience to her father's commands; then the next minute would he run out extravagantly against those mistresses that showed any kindness to their lovers, making severe reflections on their virtue and conduct. I heard him with a great deal of impatience, and interrupting his harangue, I rallied him extremely for the injustice he did Belisa and for indulging such unaccountable fancies.

He then was pleased to be very angry with me, but I let him vent his passion, and then asked him why a man might not as well quarrel with a glass that shows him an ill face, as with a friend that gave him the true representation of his soul. Octavius made no reply of a long time but kept his eyes fixed on me, when on a sudden he broke the silence, and rising up, "Well," said he, "my generous friend, you have awakened something in my soul, and the eyes of my understanding begins to be cleared. Proceed then," continued he, "and use your utmost skill to cure me of this outrageous passion jealousy that defies prudence and reason. I own it is a weakness; but if it be possible, let me conjure you to rid me of this strange malady."

I was glad to find he had a sense of his extravagant passion; and having some esteem for him, as he was a relation to Lysidas, I replied that I would endeavour to approve myself his friend; that I would do nothing by halves, for since it was a continual spring of industry, that I would use my utmost skill to extinguish his unreasonable surmises wherewith I found him so cruelly tormented, and perhaps I might discern better than he, what was most to his advantage. Octavius thanked me a thousand times and promised me he would add his own endeavours to my care, to be cured of his madness. And I doubt not but he used his utmost effort. But this disease had taken so deep a root in his heart that his reason was of little use when the frenzy fit was on him, for he would create afflictions on purpose to make himself unfortunate.

About a week after this discourse happened, he was to wait on Lysidas; and when I had an opportunity, I demanded of him if it was possible to love without jealousy. "Alas! Madam," replied this unhappy lover, "I am not yet cured of my weakness; for this unaccountable humour has that ascendant over me that were the best physicians of all parts of the world assembled together, they would in vain endeavour to dislodge this disease, which occasions so much mischief and which is irreparable because, instead of seeking remedies, false praises are generally invented to flatter it."

"You speak so feelingly of your distemper," said I to Octavius, "that I hope you will attribute your cure more to your own reason than to any arguments I can use. But still let reason stand sentinel at your heart; for this jealousy will certainly find entrance there, if watch be not well guarded. 'Tis the most fatal of all the passions; 'tis a complication of all the evils in the world; 'tis the fury of furies."

"But did you love as I did," replied Octavius, "you would not be so great an enemy to jealousy. However, I will endeavour to chase from my heart a passion so pernicious to my repose. Your conversation has so far convinced me that I must allow that those lovers are most happy and most rational that can love without jealousy, or only so little to keep up the flame." And for two months I had the glorious title of physician for curing a disease that was thought above all rules of medicine; but the fit returned with greater impetuosity than before.

As Octavius was one day at cards with Belisa, she accidentally let fall her cards two or three times, and a young spark that sat next her was very obsequious in taking them up, and, out of a piece of gallantry, would kiss the cards as he gave them to her. As she received them she smiled and said that she was ashamed of the trouble she gave him. To which he replied that he should ever after love the cards that had given him an occasion to render her a small piece of service. Though only these common compliments passed between them, yet Octavius could not bear it, but relapsed into his former capricious fancies. His reason was of no use to him, so blindly he abandoned himself to his passion, which was then the most predominant in his soul; and the uneasiness he was in was so visible to all the company, that Belisa left off cards and retired herself into her closet, where she made vows to herself never to see him more. For now she had lost all hopes of ever being happy with him; wherefore she made it her request to her father to forbid him his house, who in complaisance to his daughter did as she desired, which so enraged Octavius, that he was like a man distracted (for he loved Belisa passionately) and being ashamed of his folly, would never see me more. But he sent me word by Lysidas that though his disease still continued to plague him, he thanked me for the care and application I had used to cure him. Upon this business he went out of town and sought his relief amongst a savage, unbred sort of two-legged brutes in Wales, where he lived a very solitary life.

I have insisted upon the particulars of Octavius, my dear Indamora, to let you see that jealousy is a disease seldom to be overcome. Therefore acquaint your friend Clorinda with this story, and the influence you have over her may prevent her marriage with the jealous Melicrates; for let the wife be never so virtuous, the jealous-pated husband is ever full of disquiets for fear his horns should not fit easy on his head, when at the same time he is laying snares to trepan his neighbour's pretty wife. But the golden rule of doing as you would be done unto is banished from amongst us.

Before I finish my letter, I must add that I received a confirmation of Cleomidon's intentions of being in town as he designed, but that his uncle and aunt reproached him with too soon forgetting his Cleodora and were both much offended at him, but that should not deter his intentions; for his only happiness was in my company. This assurance of his kindness still more augmented my good fortune, and I thought it long till I could behold my faithful Cleomidon. In my next you shall participate of my joys; but at present I can add no more than to assure you, I am

My Indamora's

Sincere friend and servant,

Lindamira

Letter XX

That day, my dearest Indamora, that I expected Cleomidon in town preceded the happy night wherein Elvira gave so much joy to the Colonel in bringing him a fine boy into the world. To deal sincerely with you, I was very unwilling to accompany Doralisa to Elvira's, fearing in my absence Cleomidon might come to town, as I expected. I suffered some inquietudes upon his account, for he came not till three days after the time he allotted, which possessed me with an unusual fear; and my heart foreboded some ill fortune to him. And indeed my conjectures were not ill-grounded; for the last day's journey he was overturned in his coach and, falling, unfortunately broke his right arm, which detained him three days on the road, but was so happy to meet with a good chirurgeon, who set it so well that in three days he left the inn where he was advised to continue for some longer time; but, as he told me, his desire of seeing me after so long an absence made him so impatient, that he resolved to comply with his inclinations and not with the advice of his chirurgeon.

That night he came to town, he sent his servant to acquaint me with his arrival and of the unlucky accident that detained him on the road, and to beg excuse for not writing or waiting on me. His indisposition easily sealed his pardon, and I was extremely afflicted at his misfortune. The next day Doralisa and I went to see him. We found him laid on his bed, fast asleep (for he had not slept all the night past), but he soon awoke and, seeing us by his bedside, seemed much amazed. He expressed to us the most obliging acknowledgments that a grateful heart could imagine, and 'tis impossible to express the transports of joy he showed, as he said, for the favour we did him. He so overvalued the least marks of my esteem, that I could not reproach myself from being too sensible of his affection. Our joys were both so great and so tumultuous, that of a long time I did not think to ask him what life he led since our fatal separation.

"Then know, my dearest Lindamira," said Cleomidon, "that a month after I married, I went into the country with Cleodora; but we were obliged to live with the cruel Lyndaraxa, who you have heard did wheedle my uncle to marry him. This couple were of as different humours as their interest; and though Alcander adored his money and loved it entirely, yet his design was to make me happy with Cleodora and to settle her a jointure answerable to her fortune. But Lyndaraxa, whose sentiments were different from those of Alcander's, diverted the execution of his intention on purpose to bring about her own hellish plots. She was esteemed by some to be a woman of wit and great sense; but, alas, she so ill employed her wit, that her genius was only to circumvent her husband in whatever he designed. And I will do her this justice as to say her person was agreeable, and her wit very taking when she was in the humour to be good company. She seemed inclined to melancholy and to be very studious, and applied herself much to reading. This gave her the reputation to be a woman of a sound judgment, and, having a happy memory, would relate what she had read so perfectly that her auditors had a great pleasure in heark'ning to her. But the sequel of my discourse will best demonstrate how ill she employed her talent, and that her wit and memory was of no other use than to abuse those who had too good an opinion of her. And amongst others, I had as high thoughts of her virtues as anyone, till by accident I made a happy discovery of her perfidy and treachery."

Cleomidon had continued his discourse had not his physician come in, who put a stop to the sequel of this adventure which had so raised my expectation. But fearing a longer visit might be injurious to his health, we took our leave for that night; but Cleomidon failed not to acknowledge this favour, and told us that the next day he would wait on us and finish what he had yet to acquaint us with.

From thence we went to see my amiable friend, Elvira, who was then in a happy way of recovery, and much delighted and pleased that she had an heir to inherit so good an estate. We passed that evening with her, and she easily read in my countenance the satisfaction I received in having seen Cleomidon. As she was no stranger to this adventure, I did not scruple to acquaint her of his being in town. Upon this relation, she said a thousand obliging things to me that testified how great a part she bore with me, and expressed a great curiosity to know in what Lyndaraxa had forfeited the good opinion the world had of her: for, said Elvira, "I knew one of her character, who deceived all that knew her, and, being conscious of her own evil intentions, was jealous that all her friends took her for a hypocrite, but at the same time made great protestations of sincerity and, by a mild affected way, deluded those who thought themselves entirely acquainted with her humour."

" 'Tis so frequent," replied Doralisa, "to meet with persons who profess much goodness and practice little, that I am not astonished at it; but her whom Elvira has mentioned is for certain my Lady —" "Hold," said Elvira, "for I would not rake the ashes of the dead, and so will bury in silence those unhappy qualities of a lady of her reputation."

We took leave that night of Elvira, and the next day I received a visit from Cleomidon; but the sequel of his story I refer to my next letter.

I am,

My dearest Indamora,

Your entirely affect. servant,

Lindamira

Letter XXI

In this manner, my dearest Indamora, Cleomidon continued his narrative.

"Know then, Lindamira," said he, "that it was whispered about that Lyndaraxa was with child; and when her friends congratulated with her, she seemed to deny it in such a manner that more confirmed them in that belief; but, in a short time after, it was visible to all the world, and my uncle was extremely pleased at it: and though the consideration of my interest would have allayed my joy, yet I bare a part with my uncle in the satisfaction he had. But one day as I was sitting in a back parlor that a door opened into the garden, I was reading very studiously and did not, of a long time, take notice of any one thing under the window; but hearing myself named awoke me from the consideration of what I was a-reading, and raising up my head, I saw Lyndaraxa and a gentlewoman with her, who were both in very earnest discourse. But, as I told you, having heard myself mentioned, it raised a curiosity in me to hearken to them. 'And,' pursued Lyndaraxa, 'be sure you give me timely notice when I must begin to make faces and complain of pain; for if I can introduce a child unseen (either son or daughter) it will disappoint Cleomidon of his hopes.' The other assured her that she might depend upon her management, and that she had contrived so cunning a way to introduce the child, that there would never be any surmises that it was an imposture. I believe they had continued their discourse, had not my uncle passed through the parlor into the garden and, seeing me at the window, asked me to walk with him.

" 'Tis not to be imagined how I was astonished at the ungenerous temper of Lyndaraxa, for I did not believe her capable of so great a treachery; but as I thought it absolutely necessary to acquaint my uncle with it, I failed not that day as we were walking. The old gentleman blushed for anger and was so ashamed to be so put upon, that he expressed the highest resentments that such an affront could excite him to. That evening he taxed Lyndaraxa with the discourse she had with Sabina in the garden. She had not impudence enough to deny it; but finding her plot was circumvented, she made an ingenuous confession, and on her knees begged my uncle's pardon in such moving words and actions, adding a sincere repentance, and tears fell so plentifully from her eyes, that it so mollified Alcander's heart that he easily sealed her pardon. From that day she pretended herself not well; and her great belly being gone, it was easily suspected why she kept her chamber.

"But from that time Lyndaraxa bore me a mortal hatred, and solemnly swore to Sabina to be revenged of me the first opportunity she could find. And, on the contrary, my uncle was more kind than ever, as being conscious he had done me a piece of injustice, after the promise he had made me to settle his whole estate on me if I married to his liking; and I doubt not but he repented of his bargain. At the end of the fourteen months, Cleodora was brought to bed of a fine girl, and Lyndaraxa took an occasion to be angry it was not a son. This was to show the capriciousness of her temper; nor would she appear at the christening day, nor be godmother as she did intend had it been a son. But her absence was the least of my troubles. For her ill usage of Cleodora was an affliction to me, who often lamented the misfortune of being educated by one who took so little care to instruct her in what was most advantageous to improve her mind; but as her inclination was good and virtuous, she had nothing of the humour of Lyndaraxa, who, finding that Cleodora thought herself happy, was resolved to destroy her tranquillity by suggesting to her mind that I was in love with the fair Hermione, a young gentlewoman that often did us the honour to come and stay a week together. Her humour being brisk and airy, she very much diverted Cleodora, who naturally was melancholy. As I was sensible she came out of kindness to my wife, I often expressed my thankfulness to her; and knowing that Cleodora was very well pleased with her conversation, I took those opportunities of being in my closet; and, to confess the truth, I spent much time in thinking on you and writing to you: I complained of the rigor of my fate; I demanded your advice in a thousand little occurrences; I sent my wishes for your happiness, and for a sight of you, ten thousand more. But after all I durst not disobey you. I burnt my letters, then wrote again, then sacrificed them to the flames; and in this manner did I pass my days.

"But to return to Hermione, who was ignorant of the plots and stratagems that did surround her, one day very innocently asked me before Cleodora and Lyndaraxa why they had so little of my company. 'For,' said this pleasant lady, 'I believe you agree with the opinion of most men that women are not capable of giving a rational answer, having not the advantage of learning and reading those authors that are so improving to the mind.' But being willing to convince Hermione of that error, I said to her a thousand obliging things in favour of the fair sex, and endeavoured to let her see I was not of a humour to despise those from whom learning was not expected, and that I thought women were capable of the deepest philosophy, were it a necessary accomplishment; but they had so many advantages over us that Hermione had no reason to suspect that her company was not extreme pleasing and diverting, and that a lady of her wit and good humour ought not to have those unjust apprehensions. For an hour or two did we entertain ourselves upon this subject; and Lyndaraxa made her observations of what was said and from this innocent entertainment raised the foundation of a most detestable design. She took this occasion to represent to Cleodora how industrious I was to convince Hermione of the respect I paid to her sex, and that she observed how amorously I looked on her and that she received my kindness with a great satisfaction, and believed there was a reciprocal affection between us, that if a stop was not put to it in the beginning, she would alienate my affections from her; and Cleodora gave but too much attention to her, and being of a nature very credulous, it took the effect that Lyndaraxa desired. And finding a change in the humour of Cleodora, who was become more pensive and melancholy, I feared it proceeded from some indisposition of body; but finding it was her mind that was disturbed, I pressed her extremely, before she would discover this secret to me. But at last she frankly told me all that Lyndaraxa had suggested to her and that she bid her observe our looks, our words, and all our actions. But I so happily convinced Cleodora of the error she was in, that she begged my pardon for having such unjust thoughts of me; and from that time her mind was restored to its former tranquillity, and she more than ever esteemed Hermione.

"When Lyndaraxa finding her plot had not taken so well as she desired, she nevertheless endeavoured to make us uneasy, but it was not in her power; but she was not forgetful of the oath she had taken to Sabina to be revenged of me, which perhaps she might have effected had not death deprived me of Cleodora, who died of the new fever. Her death afflicted me very much, for I had no reason to complain of any unkindness from her, and I knew she loved me passionately; and that which aggravated my grief, I thought her death was hastened by the wilful humour of my aunt, who plied her so fast with medicines that one potion had not time to operate before they gave her another.

"Soon after her funeral rites were performed and that I had settled my affairs, I determined to come to London. But my uncle dissuaded me from it, and Lyndaraxa was outrageous; and being possessed I intended to marry again, she opposed my design with all the power she had; but finding she could not prevail, she said she would take care of the young Hermilia, my child, and not let her come under the tuition of a mother-in-law. As I had no friend to whom I could so well commit the care of this infant as herself, I let her take her own way, and Alcander has promised no care shall be wanting."

Cleomidon thus ended his narration, and I found he had been no less unhappy than myself, and I could not but sympathize with him.

And as the affliction of Cleomidon was no ways lessened by a long absence, he entertained me with the same passion as ever he had done; but as Cleodora had not been long dead and his arm not yet well, our marriage was deferred for two months. If you remember, my Indamora, you came to congratulate with me, it being reported I was married, but you never yet knew the reasons that hindered it.

Cleomidon was no sooner well and had left off the scarf wherein he carried his arm, but by the consent of all my relations and the approbation of those friends that held the greatest rank in my esteem, as well as by the obligations I had to be grateful, I consented to be married to him. The day was set, and my wedding clothes made; and as I was trying of 'em on, an accident happened that proved of ill consequence to me and extremely afflicted me, and that was the death of Elvira, who unfortunately had taken cold in her lying-in, which cast her into fever and in few days deprived her of life. I was so much troubled for the death of this lady that Cleomidon had much ado to comfort me; and Lysidas and Doralisa going into mourning, they obliged me to do the same. And as I had a great esteem for Elvira, I really mourned for her, and for one month I resolved to defer my marriage.

But fortune was not yet tired with persecuting of me, and she had something in reserve to complete my misfortunes. Cleomidon still continued his assiduous visits to me, and he failed not a day wherein he did not see me. How often would he expatiate on his former life, aggravating the least circumstance that might raise a compassion in my soul, and lamented his precipitate resolution in obeying Alcander, and did me that justice as to say he never had reason to complain of any baseness from me. But I cannot think on the change in his affections without suffering o'er again those disquiets my soul was agitated with; and Cleomidon, to whom I had given the title of faithful, constant, and generous, forfeited that name and approved himself unworthy of my affections.

This character, my Indamora, I am certain will surprise you, as much as I was at the news of his sudden departure out of town, which gave me so great tremblings of the heart, that I was much disordered at it; and though his pretence seemed plausible and justifiable, yet my prophetic soul suggested to me sad omens from his manner of going. And though it was his custom to see me every day, yet I took no notice to be concerned that I had not seen him of a whole day; and the next day I received a letter from him with only these few words in it.

Pardon me, my dearest Lindamira, for not waiting on you before I went out of town. The suddenness of my departure you will excuse when I tell you my uncle lies a-dying, and has sent an express for me. The few moments I have to stay are employed in assuring my Lindamira, I am,

Her faithful Cleomidon

By the first post I will not fail to write to you, and shall hope from your goodness an answer.

This letter both surprised and troubled me; but not knowing what judgment to make, I waited impatiently for the first post-day, wherein I expected a letter from him; but I not only failed of my expectation that time but several days besides. At last I concluded Cleomidon was sick, if not dead; but I wrote to him three or four times, but no answer would he return; and that which aggravated my affliction was that I heard by a gentleman (whom Lysidas, unknown to me, had sent into the country where Cleomidon lived to know what was become of him) that he was well in health but seemed very melancholy, which was ascribed to the death of Cleodora, that he had also seen the young Hermilia, that Cleomidon was very fond of her and was often heard to say he never would have any wife besides Hermilia. This news troubled me extremely, for I plainly saw he openly condemned me; but I took a resolution not to complain, fearing it should increase his pride, did he but know how great my resentments were.

I endeavoured all I could to disguise that grief that did too sensibly touch my heart, but all my endeavours were fruitless, for my eyes too plainly showed my discontent; and that which aggravated my sorrow more was that all the world knew I was abandoned by one whom I designed to marry; and several conjectures were made upon this occasion, every one to their fancy. But though I was thus unkindly used, yet love filled my heart, and all my anger could discover to me no other fault Cleomidon had but inconstancy. But why he was so, after such proofs that he had given of an unalterable fidelity, cast me into a labyrinth of thought. But the more I did consider of it, the more I was perplexed. As for jealousy, I was sure he had no cause; or if he were so, he could not disguise it from me. And being thus disturbed, and never hearing from him, I took a resolution to leave the town awhile, to try if the fresh air could disperse those clouds of melancholy that were too visible in my face, and to remove that tyrant love that monopolized all my thoughts. This design I did communicate to Doralisa, who unwillingly consented to my removal and deferred it for some time.

But surely, my Indamora, one vexation never comes alone; for, much against my will, I made another conquest when least I did expect my eyes should do such feats, and I believe you'll be surprised when I acquaint you it was Colonel Harnando, who wrote to me several most passionate letters; and though I returned all back but the first (and some unopened), yet this hero would not be repulsed, but laid close siege to my heart and was resolved upon the conquest of it. But my soul was in no frame to receive with pleasure the greatest proof of passion could be given; for I would not be deluded again, so resolved never to love, and since Cleomidon could prove untrue, I thought the whole sex was capable of change. And being unwilling to give any occasion of discourse of my being courted by Harnando, I stole out of town; and none but my two cousins and yourself knew of the place of my retreat; and though it was not far from the town, yet extreme solitary, and agreeable to my humour. The house was but small, and a garden and orchard proportionable to it, and at a little distance from the garden was a grove of chestnuts and walnut trees, where by accident I discovered a most surprising echo. This place was of great entertainment to me, for to amuse and please my fancy I often would call on the name of Cleomidon. 'Twas music in my ears to hear his name reverberated; and for that reason would often entertain myself for hours together, repeating sometimes those flattering expressions that he so freely gave. But surely love is a madness, and they that are so take a pleasure in being mad, and at that time think that a charm which, when their reason is returned, they think a misery.

Thus for a month did the time glide away in this sort of entertainment; and reason began to take place of that dullness that clogged my brain, and I grew sensible I was to blame to cherish a passion for one whom I did believe did ne'er bestow a thought on me. I therefore did endeavour to cast him from my heart, and his idea appeared to me ill-shaped, deformed, decayed, full of inconstancy and treachery. But time is at last our best friend, for he does more than reason or the best arguments in philosophy. And being thus reinstated to my former tranquillity of mind, I could think upon Cleomidon without resentment, and a cold indifference took place of all my love. And being, my Indamora, thus happily composed, I'll bid you adieu before I change to another scene; for you may observe, here's great variety in my adventure. I am,

My dearest Indamora,
Your faithful humble servant,
Lindamira

Letter XXII

I had not enjoyed myself in this solitude two months, my dearest Indamora, before I was visited by the Colonel, who, by some unlucky adventure, had found out the place of my retreat; but I was much surprised to see him as I was one day in the grove and, according to my usual entertainment, was repeating the name of the faithless Cleomidon.

"Ah! Madam," said Harnando (after the first ceremonies were over), "can you take pleasure in repeating the name of a perjured lover who cannot merit a thought from you?" I replied that the remembrance of his infidelity was the best defence I could find against a second engagement, and that the name of Cleomidon was not hateful to me, though he was ungenerous. "Then is it possible, madam," replied the Colonel, "for you still to love an inconstant, faithless wretch who values himself upon making you unhappy?" He failed not to extol my few virtues, on purpose to undervalue those of Cleomidon. He entertained me much with his own passion, and showed a mighty eagerness to have me marry him. His offers of settlements were very advantageous; for he gave me the freedom to make my own terms, if I pleased. Though I had no reason to doubt of the reality of his love, yet I could not forget that inconstancy is a disease as epidemical in that sex as 'tis believed to be in ours; but we have not that strength of parts and courage, as is natural to theirs, to support us under afflictions;

and the thoughts of being once deserted made me deaf to all the arguments the Colonel used to persuade me to be his. But all the repulses I gave him would not make him retreat, but the more opposition he found, the more vigorous he was to pursue his design of gaining my heart, which was not a conquest worthy of his pains and trouble. However, being blinded by his passion, he could see no faults I had but too much obstinacy, of which he often accused me. But the frequent visits he made I feared would be prejudicial to my reputation, which made me think of leaving my solitude sooner than agreed with my inclination.

I returned to London in ten weeks after I had left it and was frequently visited by the Colonel, and few doubted but there would be a match between us. As he was a very accomplished person, it was impossible not to be pleased with his conversation. And one day as he was with me, a servant brought me a letter that came by the post; I knew the hand to be that of Cleomidon's, but had not so much presence of mind as to disguise my surprise, for Harnando presently suspected the truth, and his countenance changed, and he looked much disturbed at this adventure. I still kept the letter in my hand, looking on the superscription as if I doubted from whence it came, for the characters seemed not so clever as those which Cleomidon generally writ; but I knew the seal too well to be in doubt. "Madam," said the Colonel, perceiving the disorderly motions of my mind, "your patience is without precedent. Methinks you are very dilatory in the perusal of what your faithful Cleomidon has sent you." He spoke this in a tone that sufficiently expressed his sense to the contrary. I made him no reply but withdrew to a window; but none can represent the unartful pantings of a faithful heart unless they've loved like me. I opened this letter, with hopes that Cleomidon was convinced of his ingratitude and had repented of his crime. But alas! I found to my sorrow that his thoughts were alienated from me; and I had hardly power to finish the reading of this letter that was so surprising to me; nor could I scarce believe my own eyes that Cleomidon should send me word of his own marriage, and in so triumphant a manner as you will find by what follows.

CLEOMIDON TO LINDAMIRA

MADAM,

Your marriage with Colonel Harnando will justify mine with the charming Hermione, to whom I have given my heart entirely. I have (though with some trouble) forgot your infidelity, and your falsehood has absolutely extinguished in my heart that love I had for you. You have taken the most becoming care in the world to let me know of your happiness, and though I could expatiate on your ingratitude, I'll bury in silence my most just resentments.

Farewell Cleomidon

'Tis impossible to express my first thoughts and apprehensions of this marriage, for this second engagement was more terrible to me than the first. For though he married Cleodora, it was through my persuasions, which out of a sentiment of generosity I argued with him for his own advantage; but to think that Hermione was possessed of what I had so tender an affection for most tore my heartstrings, and I could not bear with patience the thoughts of his second marriage. For though I thought he was become indifferent to me, yet in this emergency I found he had taken but too deep a root in my heart; nor could I pardon his inconstancy though he was sure I had been married to Harnando, for whilst Cleodora was living, for his sake I would never engage myself in any conversation where love was mentioned. But alas, my Indamora, Cleomidon did not observe those niceties, but on the contrary used me unkindly; would never answer my letters nor send me word of his intentions, but left me under pretence that his uncle was a-dying and had sent to him, when his business was to court my rival. A thousand distracted thoughts tormented me, and I knew not what to judge, if this was a banter or a reality.

But all this while, the Colonel observed the motion of my eye and the change of my countenance, which made him conclude that what I read displeased me very much. "Confess, madam," said he, "is not Cleomidon unfaithful? And can he pretend to love like me?" I only answered him with my tears, for my grief had taken away the use of my speech, and I was not able to speak one word. In the interim, Doralisa entered the room and demanded of me the cause of my grief. I gave her the letter, and went from her into my own chamber, and flung myself down upon the bed, uttering the most bitter complaints that my sorrow could inspire me with. But during my absence the Colonel took the liberty to read my letter, who was as much surprised at the news and manner of sending it as I was myself, and was much amazed that it should be reported he was married to me, since all the rhetoric he could use would not prevail with me to part with my dear liberty. He told Doralisa he was now in hopes I would the sooner confirm the faithless Cleomidon in the report and dispose of myself as he had done, assuring her that 'twas impossible for man to love with a more sincere affection than he did. He took his leave of her, and his countenance expressed a secret joy that Cleomidon was married.

In this extremity of trouble, what should I have done if Doralisa by her advice had not mollified my resentments? To her I unloaded all my sorrows, and in her breast I buried all my griefs. This dear kind friend at last persuaded me to dry up my tears, telling me that perhaps it might be a counterfeit letter, unless the constitution of his soul were altered, and that if I please to be convinced of the truth, she would oblige Martillo, Lysidas his friend, to go into the country to know the certainty of it. But I would not consent to it, but said I would endeavour to despise him that could use me thus ungenerously, and knowing his hand and seal so well, I could not be deceived. And then came floating into my memory the jealousy that Cleodora had of Hermione, believing there was cause for it and that Cleomidon had deceived me in the relation of that adventure. This thought raised storms of anger in my breast, and I could not forgive his falsehood.

Doralisa and I consulted a long time what might give the occasion of this report of my marriage with Harnando, or what could oblige Cleomidon to such a silence, never to answer any of my letters; nor could he be jealous of the Colonel, who had not made his first visit to me, after the death of Elvira, for three weeks or a month after the departure of Cleomidon; so that weighing all things, I was confirmed that it was the sickliness of his temper and that the beauty of Hermione had made him forget all his vows to me. This perjured wretch I thought once to have writ to, and have justified myself; but that thought was soon diverted with this consideration, that he was married and it would signify nothing. I then used my utmost efforts to banish him from my thoughts, and would not suffer Doralisa to mention his name to me.

Two days after, the Colonel came to visit me; he was so generous not to triumph o'er my misfortune, nor did he aggravate the inconstancy of Cleomidon, but only said that the choice of our condition was not always in our power, and that neither the counsels of our friends nor that of our reason could engage our minds, but that we were carried on by the violence of a passion that is irresistible. After this manner did he entertain me, and suffered some days to pass before he spoke any more of love to me. But one day as he was with me, I discovered a dullness upon his countenance, which I thought must proceed from some great cause, and asked him how his little son did, fearing he might be ill. He replied that his son was well, but . . . and made a stop. And being curious to know the signification of this "but" I asked the Colonel what ill news he had heard, and what did so disturb his mind. He replied that this morning he had received his commission, and had orders to go for Flanders in fifteen days. He imparted this news to me with so great a concern and trouble, that I had reason to believe I was partly the cause of his sorrow. He failed not to tell me as much, making a thousand protestations of his love and sincerity, and said that he loved me from the first time he ever conversed with me, and that neither time nor absence could deface the impression I had made upon his soul; that unless I made him some returns of love, he was, of all men, the most miserable. And not being insensible of my obligations to the Colonel and that I knew he merited a nobler fate than what he so earnestly sought after, I failed not to assure him of the esteem and acknowledgment I had for him, but the condition of my soul was such that I could not retaliate love for love, but if he could content himself with my friendship, he should find it sincere and lasting.

These few civil words drew from his mouth a thousand assurances of his fidelity; and being in hopes that friendship in time might ascend to love, he seemed more satisfied than before. And to own the truth, the thoughts of his departure gave me more trouble than I imagined it could; knowing the uncertainty of a battle, the fatigue of a campaign, and what hazards he must perpetually run, that I discovered my concern both by my looks and actions, which gave him hopes he was not so indifferent to me as a few days before he feared he was. His visit was not long that day, being obliged to give his orders about his departure; and, as he was going, "Tell me, madam," said he, "what consolation may an absent lover find when separated from the object of his affections? May he hope he shall one day be happy, if he returns victorious over his enemies? These thoughts," continued he, "will charm the fleeting hours away; and the hopes that Lindamira's love will be my recompense will so animate my courage and redouble my force, that I promise myself the victory before I go." But since I gave him no other hopes than the continuation of my friendship, he seemed so dejected and cast down that I really pitied him. And folding his arms across, "Unhappy Harnando," said he, "where shall my distracted thoughts find ease, if Lindamira forbids me to hope? Alas!" said he, "No condition can equal mine; for I love one passionately that loves another that is perjured, unfaithful, and unworthy of her."

I endeavoured what I could to appease his passion and to represent to him how much he offended me for the little value he set upon my friendship. He begged my pardon, so much exaggerating the violence of his love that I could not be angry at him.

When he was gone, I was sensible that his departure would be a trouble to me, for those admirable qualities both of body and mind claimed a respect and esteem of all that knew him; and had I been inclined to a second affection, I could not have refused Harnando the request he made me to marry him, with advantages beyond my merits. But not being willing to be fettered or enslaved by any, since the best of the whole sex had deceived me, I kept to my resolution not to marry anyone. Adieu, my Indamora.

> I am,
>
> Your affectionate friend and servant,
> Lindamira

Letter XXIII

The night before that Colonel Harnando was to go for Flanders, my dearest Indamora, he came to take his farewell of me, but with a countenance so dejected, that it grieved me extremely to see him look so sad; and believing there was some hidden cause for it, I begged to know what 'twas that troubled him. He looking earnestly on me, answered with a sigh that some envious planet interposed between him and all his hopes, that when he was absent, his rival would be happy in the possession of me. These words he spoke in so dismal a tone that it both surprised and troubled me, nor could I divine what he meant by his rival; for he knew that Cleomidon was both inconstant and married. Wherefore I asked him why he was so ingenuous at tormenting of himself, since he had no rival to fear; and that if Hermione were dead, I would never marry Cleomidon; and if I would change my condition, it should be in favour of himself, there being none I did esteem so much as him.

But this disconsolate lover seemed not satisfied with what I said, but asked me if I would promise to marry him (if death did not make an eternal separation between us) at his return. "For," added he, " 'tis not to be expressed, what my fears suggest to me; and my just apprehensions makes me suffer as great torments as if ten thousand vultures were tearing of my heart. But oh! my happy rival! He will triumph in my absence, and laugh at my misfortune!" "Who is this terrible rival," said I, interrupting of him, "that gives you so great a fear? Explain your meaning, and I may rectify your mistake." "You will but too soon know, madam," said he, "whom I fear and whom I dread; but pardon me, that I say no more." He then rose up to take his last adieu, begging of me not to forget him, to write to him, and to receive his letters kindly. I promised him what he desired, nor could I forbear some tears at our separation, which I thought a just tribute due to his merits. Thus did the poor Colonel take his leave of me, desiring I would sometimes see his son, which might perhaps call into my memory the unhappy father.

The absence of so worthy a friend gave me some disturbance, and I could not think of his last words without grief and trouble; nor could I apprehend the meaning of those ambiguous words he spoke. By the first opportunity I had an account of his safe arrival. I answered his and received several others, which were writ with all the passion imaginable and in a most pathetic strain; for none could express their thoughts more elegantly than himself. Our correspondence continued punctually for some months on both sides; for the Colonel never failed to write to me as often as he had opportunity or his affairs would permit. It was never my humour to be inquisitive after news; yet for his sake sometimes I would inform myself of the movements of both armies, and passes lost and won. But this curiosity gave me some disturbance, as one night I was at supper, and some gentlemen discoursing with Lysidas of the affairs of Flanders, lamenting the death of some of their friends, I unhappily asked if they had heard any news of Colonel Harnando. One of them answered, that by the last post he heard he was wounded by a bullet shot into his neck and that some despaired of his recovery. This news was the more surprising, having had a letter from him but two posts before; but the disorder it cast in my thoughts was seen by my eyes, which Lysidas perceiving, endeavoured to divert my fears by saying there were many false reports raised, on purpose to afflict them who had any friends in this last expedition.

As soon as supper was ended, I retired with Doralisa into my chamber, where we both lamented the unhappy fate of the Colonel; but being willing to hope it was only a flying report, we endeavoured to comfort ourselves but, the next day had the news confirmed to our great sorrow. But two posts after, I received a letter from Leander, a friend whom the Colonel had intrusted with the secrets of his love, to give me an account of his health, which was then in a very bad condition; but in a short time after, he made a shift to write to me himself, though he lay very ill of his wound, desiring I would continue writing to him; and withal he raised my hopes that his life was in no hazard. But no sooner was my mind resettled for the danger the Colonel had been in, but a new and most surprising adventure befell me.

You may remember I have formerly mentioned Martillo to you, Lysidas's friend, whose business called him to Byzantem, a town in the same county where Cleomidon lived. It happened at that time there was a horse race, where a piece of plate of two hundred pounds was to be run for, which brought all the gentlemen of the country thereabouts to be spectators of this sport, and amongst the rest, Cleomidon. Martillo seeing of him (at whose house he had formerly dined) took the freedom to wish him joy of his new lady. At these words Cleomidon started and desired him to explain himself, saying he was never married to any but Cleodora, who had been dead near fifteen months. "Is that possible," replied Martillo, "and are not you married to the fair Hermione?" " 'Tis certainly so," said Cleomidon; "for Hermione had been married these three months, and there you may see her husband," pointing to a gentleman that stood near him. "But, sir, you so surprise me with this news that I must beseech you to tell me where you heard it." "This place," replied Martillo, "is not at all proper to discourse of it; for much depends upon the truth of Hermione's not being married to yourself. And when the race is over," said this friend, "I will meet you where you shall appoint; for perhaps it may be in my power to do you a small service." Cleomidon complied with Martillo, and as soon as the sport was over, they met according to appointment.

"The consternation you have put me in," said Cleomidon, "is not to be expressed, nor can I imagine what could occasion so false a report; for she is a lady I never pretended to." "No, sir?" said Martillo. "Then why did you write to a lady you had formerly courted, that you were now married to the charming Hermione?" "Alas! Sir," said Cleomidon, "what you tell me amazes me; and explain this enigma, to deliver me out of the pain I suffer; for my heart forebodes some treason has been contrived against me to destroy my happiness. And if 'tis possible, clear all my doubts, and let me know every circumstance has been related that has confirmed this flying report."

"The first news of your marriage," said Martillo, "I heard at a coffeehouse you did usually frequent when you were in town; but it was confirmed under your hand and seal in a letter to Lindamira—" "Hold," said Cleomidon. "Do you know Lindamira? And did she receive a letter from me that mentioned my marriage with Hermione?" " 'Tis most assuredly so," replied Martillo, "and the letter I have seen and read over several times, and I believe my memory has retained it all, or great part of it"; and, at Cleomidon's request, repeated it to him.

But the surprise Cleomidon was in, at the recital of this letter, is not to be expressed. For a long time he kept silence, with his eyes fixed on the ground; then lifting of them up to heaven, as to bear witness of his innocence, "Oh most unhappy Cleomidon!" said he. "Was ever constant lover so much abused, or ever so great a villainy contrived to make me the most wretched of mankind! How much am I become the loathed, detested object of Lindamira's thoughts, whose just resentments nothing can appease! For could she believe me married to Hermione, and yet preserve a friendship for me? Oh, no! She has revenged herself on me and made Harnando happy."

"How do you mean, happy," said Martillo, interrupting of him, "since the Colonel is now in Flanders?" "This letter," replied Cleomidon, showing it to Martillo, "has been the cause of my misery. And nothing but Lindamira's own hand could have persuaded me she could have loved another."

Martillo, taking the letter from him, read these words.

LINDAMIRA TO CLEOMIDON

You will not wonder I have changed my sentiments, when you know 'tis in favour of Colonel Harnando, on whose kindness depends all my happiness, which I esteem beyond the western mines. What has passed between us, let be buried in oblivion, as shall the memory of Cleomidon, by

Lindamira

Martillo, having read the letter with wonder and amazement, returned it Cleomidon, telling him that never so black a treason was contrived to make two persons so unhappy, whose hands were so well counterfeited that anyone might be deceived; but yet he could not comprehend the meaning of his sudden departure out of town, and why he never answered Lindamira's letters.

"That which occasioned my journey out of town," replied Cleomidon, "I imparted to Lindamira, my uncle then being extreme ill, as my friend wrote me word, urging many specious reasons for my immediate departure. That night I arrived at my house, I wrote to Lindamira that I would not fail to be in town by that time our nuptials were to be celebrated, unless she commanded the contrary; for my uncle was very ill of a fit of the gout. I impatiently waited her answer; but not hearing from her, I wrote again and gave her an account of all my designs, begging of her by all our loves not to fail writing to me. But having thus drilled on a fortnight, I became very melancholy, not knowing what to conjecture; and as ill as my uncle was, I desired he would give me leave to go away, for I feared some misfortune had befallen Lindamira, that I had not heard from her. And Lyndaraxa maliciously replied that she heard she had so many admirers, that she feared I should have the least share of her heart. But however, I resolved to be gone in two days. And, unfortunately, the day before I assigned for my departure, two gentlemen dined at my house that was newly come from London; and Lyndaraxa, who was always inquisitive after news, demanded of one of 'em, what was the best news in town. He replied that the marriage of Colonel Harnando and Lindamira was the only discourse at present. The other replied that he had soon forgot Elvira that could think of marrying so soon. The first made answer that the Colonel had a kindness for her in his lady's lifetime, who was jealous of her, and 'twas thought she laid it so much to heart that it was the occasion of her death.

"This discourse," said Cleomidon, "was like a dagger to my heart; for knowing what excellent endowments and attractions the Colonel had, it bred such a hurricane of thoughts within my breast that I was all a flaming fire, which in my labouring fancy was never at ease; nor could I taste that cordial, sleep, that helps to ease a troubled mind. The loaded prisoners with chains suffered not such torments as I did. But to embitter more my pain, the next morning I received a confirmation of this news from Lindamira's hand, and that, sir, was the letter you have read. Though now I am convinced it is a forgery, yet then I thought her false, and the most perjured of womankind. Yet however, I intended to present myself before her, only for her punishment, to observe how she could look on me after the vows that she had broke. But as my resentments were no secret, my uncle said all he could to appease me, and persuaded me not to complain to Lindamira, since her fault could not be pardoned; and Lyndaraxa cunningly advised to slight her infidelity, since nothing could so much gratify the humour of an inconstant mistress as to see her lover torment and afflict himself for her sake. Thus was I persuaded to forbear my resentments, which if I had not delayed, it would have spared me many a restless night; and had I followed the torrent of my passion, I should have known the truth, and then this veil of falsehood had been torn away, and Lindamira had appeared as innocent as ever. But now, Martillo, what may I hope? Will she be deaf to all my prayers? Will she forgive my silence, and impute my fault to my most rigorous fate?"

Thus did Cleomidon complain, which moved so much compassion in Martillo that he promised to serve him to the utmost of his power, and would prepare my mind to hear his story. They appointed a day to be in London; but Cleomidon's impatience brought him a day sooner than Martillo.

My ignorance of what I have now related made me commit so great an absurdity that I can hardly forgive myself; but what I have more to say will make this letter too voluminous; therefore I will conclude this, with the assurance of my sincere love to my dearest Indamora.

I am, your faithful
Lindamira

Letter XXIV

Cleomidon was no sooner come to town, my dearest Indamora, but he came directly to Lysidas's house and demanded
if I were at home, and being told I was, begged the favour to
be admitted to me. This news was very surprising, and I much
admired how he durst approach me after the injustice he had
done me; but he being totally cast out of my favour, I sent
him word I had company with me and could not see him.
This message did not much surprise him, knowing by Martillo how great my resentments were, but he sent a second
time, in the most submissive terms imaginable, saying he had
something of importance to discover to me that related to us
both. But this I thought only a pretence to see me, and no excuse could justify his base actions; that I sent him word again
I would never see his face, and wondered how he could desire
to see mine. These last words made him almost distracted;
and I had the pleasure of seeing him in all the transports of
grief and trouble (for there was a window on the stairs that
looked into the parlor, that I could see anyone and not be
seen). Thus did I please myself in tormenting of him; for at
that time no flinty rock was more hardy and inaccessible than
my heart, and though Iris interceded much in his behalf and
begged of me to see him, yet nothing could prevail, and a
third time I sent word absolutely to forbid him ever to come
where I was.

This last message was like a thunderbolt to his heart, which cast him into that despair and transport of grief that of a long time he spoke not a word. At last said he to Iris, "Will you tell the cruel Lindamira that I will obey her, but 'tis barbarous in her not to hear my justification. I have such things to acquaint her with that will startle her belief; but I will leave the rest to Martillo, who perhaps may have more credit with her than I have." As he ended these words he immediately went away, with looks so dejected and so pale, as if his grave he intended should be the place of his asylum.

But he was no sooner gone but I repented, and wished I had but seen him, to have upbraided him with his infidelity; but in this emergency I knew not what to do, for Doralisa was gone out, whose advice I wanted very much.

As soon as my two cousins were come home, I acquainted them with this wonderful news, which extremely surprised 'em, and they wished I had granted Cleomidon an audience, believing it possible for him to have appeased my resentments and that perhaps he had been treacherously dealt by. This thought made Lysidas very industrious to find out his lodging (for he infinitely esteemed Cleomidon, and his baseness to me was a great grief to him, as believing him incapable of such an action), but his endeavours were fruitless. That evening, Martillo came to town and, not meeting with Cleomidon according to appointment, came to Lysidas's house and acquainted him with what had passed between him and Cleomidon at Byzantem. He related all that I have already mentioned to you, which rejoiced Lysidas beyond what can be imagined. And when Martillo told me this adventure, which he did with so much seriousness that I could not doubt the truth, I was ready to faint away, and I found myself dispirited; for I was so extremely affected with the relation of Cleomidon's innocence and vexed at my own ill nature for not letting of him see me, that I wanted no other accuser but my own conscience. But as I was ignorant of what was past, I did but serve him as he deserved. But however, I excused myself to Martillo, who told me that the hour of their appointment was come and demanded of me if I would not send some words of consolation to the unhappy Cleomidon. I desired him to tell him, as being ignorant of his innocence, he could not expect a better treatment from me; but since he had not forfeited that character that made me to esteem him, he should find me as sincerely his friend as ever.

But Martillo, instead of meeting Cleomidon, found a letter directed to him and one for me enclosed in it, which made him return with speed, saying to me that I ought to answer it, for he found by his that Cleomidon was sick. I opened it and found these words.

CLEOMIDON TO LINDAMIRA

You could let me depart, madam, without hearing my justification, which is too tedious to write; but I have been inhumanly betrayed by my most intimate friends, which has made me appear a strange criminal to Lindamira. But my innocence is equal to the love I bear you. I beseech you, permit me to make my complaint, that I may demonstrate the treason has been acted against me. And nothing but the influence of your eyes can revive me under such violent pressures I now suffer. Deny not my request to the most passionate of lovers, whose only ambition is to die.

Yours, Cleomidon

This letter wrought that compassion in my soul that I could not help shedding tears at the reading of it, which had so mollified my anger that I accused myself of barbarity, and begged a thousand pardons of Cleomidon. But Martillo, being in haste to be gone, desired that I would answer his letter kindly and that he might be the messenger of it. I therefore wrote him these few words, as follows.

LINDAMIRA TO CLEOMIDON

Your innocence has defaced out of my heart those just resentments I had against you, which were proportionable to the esteem I ever had for you. And whilst I believed you guilty of infidelity and ingratitude, I treated you like a criminal. I am impatient to hear your justification, and to know who are those treacherous friends that have so inhumanly betrayed you. Assure yourself that I am sincerely,

Your Lindamira

Martillo lost no time but went to Cleomidon's lodging, where he found him sick in bed, and his physician with him. "This is kindly done," said he, "to come and see a dying friend; and by this I find you have received my letter, but what reception the enclosed found I dread to hear." "Fear nothing," replied Martillo, "for Lindamira's heart is not so inflexible as you had reason to believe. The relation I have given her of your past misfortunes has so mollified her heart that she gave me this letter for you, and does also desire you to be careful of your health." Cleomidon received this letter with all the transports of love and passion, and thanked Martillo for the good office he had done him. "But my kind friend," said he, "the condition I am in will not permit me to see my Lindamira, who desires to hear my justification." "I will return to her," said Martillo, "and acquaint her with your illness, and I am persuaded that Doralisa will prevail with her to come and see you." This officious friend so well performed his part, as that evening Lysidas, Doralisa, and myself made our visit to him.

But when I came into the room, I was not able to speak one word to him, but stood like a statue with my eyes fixed on him. I looked on him with grief and sorrow, for his misfortunes had so altered him that his colour was quite gone, and a dead paleness diffused all over his face; his eyes looked dull, and a deep melancholy settled in his countenance. Whilst I was in this contemplation, Lysidas took me by the hand and asked me if I would not speak to Cleomidon. When I approached him, I was not able to utter one word, but sat me down by him and fell into a great fit of weeping. Cleomidon was much concerned to see me in this trouble, and said to me the most passionate and tender things imaginable, but I could make him no other answer but my sighs; for all our misfortunes since our unhappy separation came crowding into my thoughts, which stopped the freedom of my speech. But Doralisa, whose soul was not agitated with so many different passions as mine, begged of me to dry up my tears and to speak to Cleomidon and to know of him the history of his life since the last breach between us.

"That, madam," cries he, "will take up more time than I fear your patience will admit on or Lindamira will afford to hearken to."

"No, my Cleomidon," said I. "I can never be tired with a relation of your innocence; and though I know, partly by Martillo, you have been betrayed and that you suspect the inhuman Lyndaraxa, yet I am ignorant how you discovered the truth and who were your intimate friends that acted this perfidious part. If the relation will not be too great a fatigue in the condition you are in, let me know this night how I have been deceived by the report of your marriage with Hermione, which has given me such just cause to complain against you."

"My dearest Lindamira," replied Cleomidon, "then you may judge by your own heart what I have suffered, though in a greater degree; for the news of your marriage with Colonel Harnando so alarmed all the faculties of my soul and reduced me to that extremity of despair, that I was not fit for human society. But your commands shall be obeyed, and I will contract this narration into as narrow a compass as I can and will let you know how fortunately I made a discovery of what I am going to relate.

"As soon as I parted from Martillo from Byzantem, I returned to my own house with all the speed I could. I sent my man to Volusius, a friend of mine, that lived within half a mile of me; to him I oftentimes imparted my mind and asked his advice on several occasions, and in this emergency wanted him to communicate the most surprising and most welcome news in the world, that you were not married to Colonel Harnando, saying to him this was the most artificial piece of treachery as ever was acted that could deceive us both with a report of each other's being married; and our hands were so exactly counterfeited as to lead us into these mistakes, to believe each other guilty of the highest ingratitude imaginable. 'I am so much afflicted at it,' said I to Volusius, 'that I should wrong an innocent person, that I would give an hundred guineas to find out the author and contriver of this malicious plot. And assist me, my dear friend,' said I, embracing of him, 'in the discovery; and though I have reason to suspect Lyndaraxa, yet I cannot prove anything against her.'

"Volusius hearkened to me with the countenance of a friend, extremely interested in my misfortune; and after a long time revolving in his mind whether he ought to own the treason or seem innocent of it, but he having some remorse of conscience, he on a sudden cast himself at my feet, and the tears trickling down his eyes, in this submissive posture he besought me to hear him.

"'Sir,' said he, 'your astonishment cannot be greater than my villainy in being an accomplice in this treasonable design, which was to destroy the satisfaction and comfort of your life.' 'Heavens forbid!' said I, interrupting of him. 'Has Volusius, my friend, betrayed me? Oh, add not new afflictions to my misery, but tell me quickly what you know, and conceal not the least circumstance that can justify my innocence to the injured Lindamira.' At these words he rose up, and his dejected looks wrought some compassion for my most cruel enemy. 'Sir,' said he, 'the confusion I am in will not permit me to make any apology, nor can I offer anything to excuse so unworthy and so ungenerous an action. But not to keep you longer in suspense, know, sir, that Lyndaraxa came to me one day when you were in London and told me she had thought

of a means how to raise my fortune in the world, if I would
be ruled by her. I thanked her for her obliging care and replied I should be very acknowledging if she'd propose a way
how I may honestly advance myself. "Then be ruled by me,"
said she, "and you shall have two hundred guineas tomorrow;
and if the project succeed according to my wishes, you shall
have a hundred a year settled on you for your life, which will
raise you above the contempt of the world and gain you the
esteem of all your acquaintance."

"'These were her proposals; and without farther scrutiny
into her designs I swore allegiance to her and an implicit
obedience to all her commands, and then she explained herself to me as follows. "You may serve me," said Lyndaraxa,
"and not be unjust to your friend Cleomidon, who is going to
precipitate his ruin with a young girl at London who has neither wit, beauty, nor fortune, and he designs to marry her very
speedily. My design is only that you would write to him that
his uncle lies a-dying, who is now ill of the gout, and I know
he will obey the summons. When he is here, leave me to finish
the rest, for I will so contrive it as to break off this match,
which will be the inevitable ruin of his daughter."

"'I confess, sir,' said Volusius, 'that she had so possessed me
with this opinion that I obeyed her without reluctancy, hoping I might do you a future service. "But, madam," said I to
her, "'tis impossible to prevent Cleomidon's marriage with
Lindamira, for he loves her passionately and thinks her not
inferior to the rest of her sex." "That is only his fond opinion,"
said this crafty lady; "but do you write to him, and do afterwards as I shall direct." I promised her what she desired; and
my fortune being at a low ebb, which she knew, I was unhappily prevailed with to comply with her.

"'That night, sir, if you remember, that you come home,
you wrote to Lindamira, and Lyndaraxa intercepted your letter and with great joy brought it to me, and thus delivered
herself smiling on me, telling me that now was the time

wherein she expected the performance of my promise. "Volusius," continued she, "you must not baulk me of my designs; for if you do, I'll summon a legion of devils to be revenged of you. Take this letter," pursued this malicious woman, "and practice these characters, for there will be occasion to counterfeit this hand." These words made me start, and I would have given my life to have been excused. But she held me to my promise, threatening me with shame and punishment if I betrayed her or did not observe her directions. She made me swear a second time to be true to her interest, and like an ungrateful perfidious wretch I did agree with her, for two hundred guineas, to counterfeit what letters she pleased, and I myself went to the post-house to receive Lindamira's letters and brought them to Lyndaraxa. But it cannot be expressed the joy she showed, when she read the melancholy complaints of Lindamira for your silence. "And she shall have more reason to complain," said she, "for Lindamira shall receive no more letters from her lover." My heart relented at the reading of this letter, but I durst not discover my sentiments, her malice was so implacable.

"'And it was her contrivance to have those two gentlemen at dinner, who told you the false news of Lindamira's marriage with Colonel Harnando; and you must know further, that there was a young agent of hers at London who had a lodging over against Lysidas's house. This creature had a pension from her to observe what passed there; and by some means she came to know that Colonel Harnando had a respect for Lindamira in Elvira's lifetime, and this innocent affection she improved to her own advantage. She was so happy in her designs that this report got credit with you, and she found it stung you to the heart, which made her very pleasant when you were buried in your melancholy thoughts. But she was no stranger to what most concerned you, for her maid Julian was an eavesdropper and had often overheard us discoursing of Lindamira in Cleodora's lifetime. She was like a Mercury, for she was very expeditious in carrying to her mistress what she heard us say; and this with truth I can affirm, that I never told her anything you said to me, but what she heard I could not deny. And Julian, who always seemed so very civil and respectful to you, was a great instrument in contriving this mischief; for she, hearing you speak of Lindamira with great affection, related to her mistress, who had sworn a revenge ever since you so happily discovered her plot with Sabina in the garden — she said she would cross you in your love and make you drag your chains heavily. This she has effectually done, and I was so unworthy to assist her in the management of it. That now, sir, inflict what punishment you please,' said Volusius, 'for I am too conscious of my own treachery to hope to escape your most severe revenge; and if repentance could expiate my fault or my sorrow atone for my crime, I may hope to find you merciful.'

"He ended his narration with infinite of tears, and I believe did truly repent of his perfidiousness, but my astonishment would not give me leave to speak of a considerable time. But at last being awakened from my amazement, 'Oh heavens!' said I. 'How am I crossed, and why am I thus unjustly dealt by? I have lost Lindamira's favour forever, and though your treachery deserves immediate death, yet I will spare your life for your punishment, and you shall go along with me to London; and if ever you see Lyndaraxa's face more, expect the heaviest vengeance in the world to light on your head.' I would not let him go home to fetch those necessaries he pretended he wanted for his journey but furnished him with money and other necessary things, because I durst not trust him out of my sight, fearing he should betray me a second time and acquaint Lyndaraxa with my intentions. And two hours after midnight we departed for London. I only took with me two servants and himself, and I left Cleander (who waits on me in my chamber) to give me an account of what passes in my absence. And this day I received a letter from him, that my uncle was surprised at my sudden departure, but Lyndaraxa is almost distracted at it, for knowing that Volusius came with me, she finds she is betrayed and she knows not to whom to vent her passion; that Alcander is in great trouble about her, being ignorant of the occasion of this frenzy; she cannot sleep but walks about the house all night and hearkens at everyone's door, in hopes to have some intelligence of what I do; that she behaves herself so much like a madwoman that Alcander fears she will do herself a mischief.

"This, my Lindamira," said Cleomidon, "is what has passed since our fatal separation. And surely, madam, I deserve your pity, for no slave has dragged a more wretched life about him than myself. Though I believed you false and thought you married to Harnando, yet I adored the author of all my misery, and your idea I could not banish from my heart. I beseech you, madam, hide not from me how great a progress the Colonel has made in your heart, for he has store of charms to engage the most insensible of your sex; he is not only descended from a most illustrious family but possesses all the advantages of a sprightly wit, and his bewitching tongue never failed of success where he designed a conquest."

But it being late, I told Cleomidon I would reserve my own adventures for the next day, and make him judge of my actions, whether or no I still merited his affections. I left him to his rest, and his mind resettled and satisfied that he still held the chief rank in my esteem. Adieu, my Indamora.

I am,

Your affectionate friend
and servant,
Lindamira

The Last Letter

The next day, according to my promise, my dearest Indamora, I was to see Cleomidon, whose indisposition obliged me
to this visit. I found him much better and in a transport of
joy that there was a true reconciliation between us. "For, madam," said he, "I can think with pleasure on all the inquietudes
I have suffered, since my Lindamira does permit me again to
love her. Therefore let us no longer tempt fate, lest we should
meet with a new disappointment, for a second separation will
be death to me. And tell me sincerely if the merits of Colonel
Harnando has not defaced that impression I had once made?"
I replied that he reigned more absolute in my heart than ever,
and being truly sensible of his sufferings, it had augmented
the esteem I had for him, which would last eternally. And at
his request, I recounted to him all that had passed between the
Colonel and myself, with the same sincerity as I have done to
you, without omitting or disguising the least circumstance,
and showed him the Colonel's letters with the copies of my
own, which I brought along with me for that purpose. I told
my Cleomidon that I thought it necessary to write to the Colonel to acquaint him with his innocency, and to desire he
would do me that justice to acknowledge there there was no
engagement between us but only a reciprocal esteem and
friendship. To this purpose I wrote to him, and sent my letter
to the post-house by Cleomidon's servant. And I doubt not but

he was well enough pleased with my sincere way of dealing with him, which immediately displayed itself in the effects, for his health returned to him in a short time after.

And in the interim that I received an answer of my letter to the Colonel, an unexpected deliverance happened to Cleomidon; for Cleander wrote him word that Lyndaraxa was raving mad by fits, and when the frenzy was in her brain, she one night designed to complete her character of being a very notorious woman, attempted the murder of Alcander. But the weapon she made use of for this purpose was a rusty knife she found by chance in the buttery, that it being so eaten up with rust, it would not enter the skin of Alcander, and the thrust she gave him awoke him from his sleep, and laying violent hands on her, he held her till his servants came to his assistance, who taking of her out of her bed (when her clothes were on) shut her into a closet that had a strong lock to it, where she was to remain till Alcander could consult with his friends how to dispose of her. But she had so much sense remaining as to be sensible of her own wickedness and to know that the law could punish her for attempting the life of her husband. But during the time of this consultation, before day broke, she made her escape out of the window by the help of some new holland that lay in her closet, which she fastened to the bars of her window, and so slid down. But when Alcander came with his friends to reproach her with her villainy, they found the bird of ill omen fled, which was a great surprise to them. Diligent search was made for her, but no tidings could be heard till the next morning. And the keeper of the park brought word that he saw his mistress floating in one of the ponds, but he durst not approach her, she looked so dreadfully. Care was then taken to have her fetched from thence; and her funeral was performed with as much privacy as possible.

Alcander began to suspect that something extraordinary must be the occasion of this disturbance in her mind, and commanded Julian to acquaint him if she knew any cause for it. This wretch, seeing herself deprived of her great support and of Volusius, began to relent of what villainy she had practiced and made a sincere confession of all I have related — first of Lyndaraxa's design of introducing a false heir, by the assistance of Sabina and her contrivance; and that Lyndaraxa has sworn a revenge to Cleomidon for making the discovery; and what she had plotted with Volusius to render us both unhappy; that finding her designs discovered, it was so great a torment to her mind that in her passion she would often say she should do herself a mischief. Alcander was so much afflicted to hear this account of his wife that it redoubled his sorrow for her, and was as much enraged at the perfidiousness of Julian, whose sight he could not bear, but ordered her to be dismissed and sent back to her friends. The old gentleman was much afflicted at this accident, and wrote to Cleomidon a letter filled with the relation of his misfortunes and also begging his pardon for the injury he had done him, wishing he would be so kind to come to him for a fortnight or three weeks. But Cleomidon said he would not leave me till he had tied the Gordian knot that nothing but death can dissolve. And a few days after, I received an answer from Colonel Harnando which was in these words.

COLONEL HARNANDO TO LINDAMIRA

MADAM,

What I feared is at last come to pass, that you would be convinced of Cleomidon's innocence; I knew the truth before I left you but had not the power to tell you so myself. I must not pretend to enter the lists with so happy a rival, who first possessed your heart. But if you will leave it to the chance of war who shall possess you, I will measure my sword with him and shall think that blood well spilt that can purchase me Lindamira.

In justice to you, madam, I do acknowledge you made me no promise to be ever mine, but you were cruel in refusing your hand when you believed Cleomidon unfaithful. But my too happy rival, envied by all mankind, must enjoy you since I cannot. This unwelcome news has added much to my indisposition. If I recover of my wounds, I will see you, though happy in my rival's arms. You may sometimes think on an unfortunate lover without violating your faith to Cleomidon, who, I'm certain, has generosity enough to pity a miserable man. Ten thousand joys attend your nuptials, and may your wishes be crowned with felicity; and when you hear of my death, afford some tears to the memory of your constant and faithful

Harnando

I showed this letter to Cleomidon, and when he had read it, seemed very much satisfied, and had goodness enough to pity the Colonel and said he would answer his letter, which he did in the most obliging terms he possibly could.

And now, my dear friend, I am come to the period of all my misfortunes; and my constancy is rewarded with the best of husbands, whose affection to me makes me infinitely happy. Our sufferings has been mutual, and our resentments were equal; and we have but too much experienced what is in the power of malice to do; that no jealousy or suspicion is able to dissolve that union that is betwixt us.

But before I conclude this tedious narrative of my adventures, I must acquaint you with one thing that is material—that the poor Colonel fell ill after the receipt of my letter, and as relapses are more dangerous than the first illness, so it is proved to him; for whether he became more careless of his life or that success did not attend the medicines he used, he fell into a violent fever, and by fits was very lightheaded; and Leander, who never stirred from his bedside, heard all his extravagant expressions of his love and despair; and when he had any intervals of sense, he would be endeavouring to write to me but had not strength to finish his letter, but to Leander did communicate his thoughts and desired him to bring me a ring which he hoped I would wear in remembrance of him. In a few days after the Colonel died, and I heard not of his death till Leander related it to me. I was most sensibly touched at this accident, and I shed many tears upon this mournful occasion; and Cleomidon was so kind to partake of my sorrow, for he was really concerned for his death; and was much lamented by all that knew him. I failed not of seeing his son as long as he stayed in town, and the great resemblance he had of his father brought him often into my memory.

Thus you see, my Indamora, I was destined to be a mother-in-law, which side soever I had chosen; and I hope that the young Hermilia will find no difference between me and Cleodora, for I have the same affection for her as if she were my own; and where there is a true love to a husband, an affection naturally follows to his children. I have nothing more to add that is material; and 'tis time to deliver you from the tedious penance you have endured, though much might be said to excuse my ill performance, as not having abilities to pursue such a work that I inconsiderately undertook. I will not trouble you with any tedious apologies, but will conclude my adventures with the assurance of my sincere affection to my dearest Indamora.

I am her faithful
Lindamira

FINIS

Textual Emendations

In the following list of emendations in the present edition the reading at the left of the colon is the emendation; the reading at the right of the colon is that of the 1702 edition. Brackets indicate inserted words. About half of the emended forms were anticipated in the 1713 edition.

page 13, line 24. esteem or: on

page 23, line 1. enter: enters

page 43, line 3. vacation: vocation

page 53, line 11. [I]

page 73, line 13. as: of

page 75, line 29. no: a

page 78, line 1. him: me

page 93, line 5. [was]

page 110, line 2. two: too

page 116, line 6. [we]

page 121, line 21. think: thought

page 123, line 14. thanked me: her

page 127, line 17. settle her: him

page 129, lines 15–16. gentlewoman: gentleman

page 129, lines 18–19. be sure you give: before you gave

page 129, line 20. [if]

page 133, line 14. unhappy: happy

page 135, line 14. saw: say

page 142, line 9. for: of

page 153, line 28. Lysidas: Cleomidon

page 157, line 12. [I]

page 164, line 10. [she]